Under the Sycamore

by J. McCreary

FOR K. MCCREARY

Thank you for not thinking I was crazy when I said I wanted to write a book. Thank you for reminding me I could do it.

WILLIAM SHAKESPHERE

Hell is empty.
All the devils are here.

WARNING

This book contains scenes that could be triggers for readers who have experienced sexual abuse. As well, this content is for mature audiences.

CHAPTER ONE

EVAN

I hated moving. It was something I had done enough of as a little girl. But this move was different. This move was for the one woman who I would do anything for. I owed her that. She had done the same for me when she was still in her right mind.

My Aunt Polly was an amazing woman whom I adored, so when I got a call from her home care nurse telling me my aunt didn't want her to care for her anymore, I knew it was time. Actually, the timing couldn't have been better. I had lost my teaching job when the school levies didn't pass, and I hadn't found another school to teach at. Maybe the timing was too perfect. Aunt Polly had always been sly, so I wondered if she had a moment of clarity and fired her nurse knowing I would come take care of her.

That was a good possibility.

I packed up my apartment, selling a chunk of my furniture on Craigslist. Why was it that most of the people who answered Craigslist ads were people you would normally avoid on the street if they were walking towards you? I think my favorite was the stinky woman with the rusted minivan loaded down with her 'treasures' that may or may not have been hiding some sort of dead body.

1

Once I had sold enough of my belongings so that all I was taking with me on the five-hour car ride was my clothing and mementos I couldn't replace, I put what hadn't sold in a box on the curb with a cardboard sign that said 'FREE.' I was sure someone wanted mismatched dishes and Tupperware that had more lids than containers.

I didn't look back as I drove away from the place I had called home for the last six years. I was happy to be heading to the small farm town in rural Pennsylvania where I had so many good memories, and one not so good one. That not so good one was the reason I hadn't been there in almost twenty years. Aunt Polly never got upset that I wouldn't visit; she made the trip to see me multiple times saying she liked visiting the big city. I knew she hated it, but I appreciated her lie.

I drove into the town of Kendrick, Pennsylvania as the sky started turning those shades of orange and pink that reminded you summer was right around the corner. I had spent so many of my summers there as a kid, it seemed fitting that I would arrive there just as spring was ending. I was looking forward to spending the long, humid days out on Aunt Polly's front porch, lazily swinging on her porch swing watching the summer sunsets and the fireflies come out for the evening.

The town hadn't changed much since I had last been there except for the small coffee stand next to the farmers' market. Main Street was deserted, businesses closed for the night, all but Andy's, the local bar. The door to the dingy building was open, the interior lit in red, green, and blue lights. People hung out front, standing on the sidewalk smoking cigarettes near a row of motorcycles. At least there was some sort of nightlife. It looked interesting, to say the least.

I turned down the gravel road that led to the old farmhouse I used to love so much. Rolling down my window, I listened as the locusts and crickets sang their lullabies, the sound of an old friend. The smells and sounds of the quiet made me realize how much this place meant to me.

The house was lit when I pulled in, the front door open with the screen door shut. Just as I remembered. It was almost as if time had stopped. That was until I saw Aunt Polly come to the door. She stepped onto the porch, and the first thing I noticed was how much she had aged since I last saw her. Her once shiny, lush hair was dull and stringy. It had been silver for years, but now it was gray. Her face was still beautiful, but she looked tired, the bags under her eyes gave her the appearance of a woman who didn't get the rest she needed. Her eyes were still bright, and when she saw me, they lit up even more.

"Evan!" she squealed, coming down the porch steps one at a time.

"Hi, Aunt Polly!" I replied, the tears starting to form in my eyes. I didn't want her to see me cry. I stood a little straighter and willed my eyes to stop burning. It was time for me to be strong for her, not the other way around like it had been for so many years.

I walked towards her to meet her, and we embraced. Her frame was so small. *Why do we have to age?* Aunt Polly had been strong, fit, and active. But now? She was a frail, old woman, and I hated it.

"I am so happy you are here, sweetheart. I have been waiting and waiting for you!" she said as she grabbed my hand to drag me up the creaky steps.

The house was exactly as I remembered it, the ceilings tall and the rooms large. The entryway still had the bench with shoes lined up under it, some of them may have even been shoes that were lined there the last time I was there. The dining room to the right had the large dinner table we had never used, and it still hadn't been used judging by the coat of dust on it. The living room on the left earned its name because it was definitely lived in. The TV had Jeopardy on, the sound low, and Lucy, Aunt Polly's home care nurse, sat on the loveseat across from where Aunt Polly must have been sitting.

Lucy was a pleasant woman in her early fifties, a little on the plump side with an infectious smile. We'd never met in person but had spoken many times over the phone and video chatted. She seemed to truly care about my aunt, and I had no intentions of letting her go; I had hired her, after all. I did plan on cutting back on her services. She wouldn't need to be a live-in nurse with me there.

"Hey there, Lucy," I greeted as I entered the room. She put down the magazine she had been thumbing through and looked up, that infectious smile taking over when she saw me.

"Evan!" she exclaimed as she jumped off the loveseat and came over to me, engulfing me in a hug. Even over video chat, she came off as a hugger. I was not much of one, only with a few people, Aunt Polly being that few people. But, I let Lucy hug me. I even hugged her back.

"I didn't think you would be here until tomorrow," Lucy said as she pulled back from me. "I would have cleaned up a little better."

"No worries, Lucy." I smiled as I looked around. The place wasn't messy or dirty; it was lived in. It had always been lived in, and that was how I liked it.

Aunt Polly sat in her recliner across from the loveseat, turning up the TV and settling in. Her eyes seemed a little unfocused, and that was how I knew she was slipping away for the moment. I looked at Lucy and nodded towards the kitchen, letting her know I wanted to talk.

"Polly?" Lucy said, getting my aunt's attention. "You okay for a few? I'm going to get Evan settled in."

"Sure, Lynette, I'm going to be just fine," she answered.

Lucy and I exchanged looks before we left the room.

"Lynette is close," Lucy said as we entered the kitchen. "Last week she called me Louis."

I cringed at the mention of that name.

Shaking it off, I smiled at Lucy.

"So, you are okay with your hours being cut back?" I asked her.

"Oh yeah, it will be nice to be home every night. But, I don't want you to get overwhelmed, so if you feel like you are going that route, you call me, you hear?"

I promised her I would.

Lucy showed me where all of Aunt Polly's medications were and the schedule of when she needed to take them. She gave me a small list of phone numbers she liked to keep on hand. I looked them over, the main number for the home care service, the number for Aunt Polly's doctor, my cell, the pharmacy, a few others and two names I didn't recognize.

"Hey, who are Levi and Rex?" I asked, looking up from the list.

"Oh, Levi is Polly's neighbor. He's been a huge help, coming over to stay with Polly if I need to run somewhere. He dug out her new garden and helped her plant a few weeks ago. Just a nice guy. I'm sure he will come over soon to introduce himself. Polly just adores him," Lucy replied.

"And Rex?"

"He's Levi's buddy. Equally as nice, although his face doesn't agree. He looks scary but has a big heart."

Aunt Polly had never mentioned either of these guys, and now I was curious.

"Which house is his?"

"Who? Levi?" Lucy asked. When I nodded yes she smiled. "He bought the Richardson's house about six years ago. He came over and introduced himself to Polly, and they have been friends ever since. You will love him."

Lucy and I went over everything from what time Aunt Polly went to bed and woke up to how warm she liked her bath water. I was grateful for Lucy. She told me she wasn't going to just throw me to the wolves. She would be staying the night and helping me settle in for the next day but didn't think she would need to be there in the evenings for long.

"Remember, nights are easy," she reassured. "Polly sleeps hard, and she goes to bed early and sleeps somewhat late. Set your alarm for seven every morning, and you'll be up before her. Honestly, this is the easiest job I have ever had."

We went back to the living room and found Aunt Polly snoozing in her recliner. Lucy woke her up, helping her out of the chair and up the stairs. I followed them carrying my bag with me. Once we reached the top stair, I dropped my bag and continued down the hall to Aunt Polly's room. She went into the adjoining bathroom and shut the door.

"You can put your stuff in your room," Lucy said. "She usually takes a few minutes."

I walked down the hall, stopping in front of the guest bedroom. The room that had been mine was occupied by Lucy, and I was fine with it. That room was not one I wanted to sleep in ever again. I opened the door to the guest room and turned on the light. Aunt Polly had updated it since I was last here. The beautiful white, wrought iron bed centered against the wall was a bed I had always wanted as a little girl. She must have bought it just for me. The sight of it brought tears to my eyes.

The room was painted a crisp white with white lace curtains hanging from the window. Antique looking nightstands were on each side of the bed with delicate looking lamps, also white. The bedding was a fluffy, soft mint green, and I couldn't wait to crawl into it. The closet had no door and was empty, so I placed my bag in it and turned to leave the room.

As I walked by the nightstand closest to the door, I noticed a framed photo sitting on it. Picking it up, I saw it was a picture of Aunt Polly with twelve-year-old me on the day of her wedding. We were both smiling wide with the sun setting behind us. Aunt Polly looked so lovely, her cream-colored dress flowing in the breeze. She was happy. She had been single for so long, and when she met the new town sheriff, things changed for her.

"Oh sweetie, I'm so glad you are here!" Aunt Polly gushed when she picked me up at the train station. School was out, and I was getting ready to spend another summer with her at her house in Pennsylvania, just as I had for the last four summers. I loved coming to her house, it was so peaceful and quiet.

"Mom said you met someone?" I asked, a little jealous that I wouldn't have my aunt's undivided attention.

"I did. His name is Louis, and he is our new town sheriff. And guess what?" she exclaimed.

"What?"

"We are getting married this summer while you are here! I told him we had to wait for you to get here. I needed you to be a part of all of it, and he agreed. He cannot wait to meet you!"

Married? My mom hadn't said anything about her getting married.

"Does my mom know?" I wondered.

"Yep, and she will be here for it! Isn't this exciting?"

I smiled and told her it was. I told her I was happy for her, but I really wasn't. I didn't want to share her, especially with some guy named Louis. I already hated him.

When we pulled up to the farmhouse, I saw the sheriff's car sitting in the driveway. He was here?

The screen door opened and a large, potbellied man stepped onto the porch. He was older, probably in his fifties, and wore a pair of glasses. He had a receding hairline and pants pulled too far up. He smiled and waved as he took a drink from the can of beer in his hand. What in the world did my aunt see in this guy?

He came down the steps and helped get my suitcase out of the back of Aunt Polly's Jeep Cherokee, kissing her on the cheek before he closed the hatch. I glared at him, the man who stole my aunt from me.

"Hi Evan," he said as he smiled down at me. He smelled like drugstore aftershave.

"Hi," I replied, not wanting to talk to him.

"Your aunt has told me everything about you. I feel like we're old friends."

"Oh." That was all I could bring myself to say.

Louis looked to my aunt, obviously not sure what else to say or do.

"Let's get inside before these mosquitos eat us alive," Louis said, and he turned and walked towards the house.

9

I felt Aunt Polly take my hand and pull me back. I looked up at her.

"Evan, what's wrong? I promise you will love Louis. You have to give him a chance."

"I am just tired," I lied.

"Okay then, let's get you inside and settled into your room," Aunt Polly told me as she started towards the house. I followed behind her.

Once we were inside, I went upstairs and saw that Louis had put my bag in my room for me. I opened it up and found my pajamas. I turned around to head to the bathroom and was startled by Louis standing in my doorway.

"Sorry!" he said as he put his hands in the air in surrender. "I didn't mean to scare you."

"It's okay," I said as my heart tried to slow itself. I hadn't even heard him come to the door.

"I wanted to tell you I put a tire swing on the back of the property on the old sycamore tree. Polly says you go out there a lot when you're here."

I loved going out to that old tree. I would take a book with me and read, or a blanket and fall asleep listening to the locusts. Sometimes, Aunt Polly would go with me. We would stay until dusk, just as the fireflies came out, and we would catch them in our hands.

I didn't want Louis to go out there.

"Thanks," I replied. I grabbed my toothbrush and toothpaste out of my bag and excused myself. He let me walk by, and as I reached the door to the bathroom, I turned. Louis was still standing there watching me, his face expressionless. I walked into the bathroom and *shut the door, and for the first time ever, I locked the door to my aunt's bathroom.*

CHAPTER TWO

EVAN

I woke up when my alarm went off at seven on the dot. I got myself showered and dressed in jeans and a white T-shirt and into the kitchen thirty minutes later. Lucy was already in there.

"Good morning, Evan," she sang as she poured a cup of coffee, handing it to me. I took it happily from her and grabbed the half and half that was sitting on the counter, pouring a healthy amount into the mug. I sat at the small table and began to sip at the delicious, hot, goodness.

"Aunt Polly still asleep?" I asked.

"Oh yeah," Lucy answered as she sat across from me. "I told you she's a late sleeper. I like to be up at seven just to be sure I'm awake before her. She usually comes down already dressed, some days better than others."

My aunt had dementia. Some days, she knew exactly who people were and what year it was. Other days? Not so much.

Lucy told me what to expect on days things weren't so clear.

"You have to remind her the same things quite a few times, and most of the time she doesn't remember. She gets aggravated and then really mean. And lately? Sorry to say, Evan, but lately she is forgetting more and more."

My heart broke a little hearing that. I spoke with Aunt Polly every other day. I had talked to her when she thought it was 1999, the year she got married. She spoke about her dress and what she wanted to serve to eat for her reception. And then, in a snap, she was in the present, asking me about my teaching job at the middle school. Our phone calls made me sad every time we spoke. I was losing her, and the guilt of not coming to see her ate away at me. I just couldn't bring myself to come. The only reason I was there at that moment was that Lucy told me my aunt desperately wanted me there. She needed me, and, after everything we had been through together, I needed to be there for her.

Aunt Polly came downstairs about an hour later, dressed in a pair of old denim overalls and a short-sleeved floral top. She used to dress this way all the time when she was younger, and I loved it. She was stylish without even trying. Her long, gray hair was in a thick braid, and a headband held her bangs back. I smiled when I saw her.

"Good morning, auntie," I said to her.

She looked at me and winked as she went over to get a glass out of the cupboard. She didn't drink coffee; instead, she drank orange juice every morning, the kind with all the pulp.

Aunt Polly was with us this morning.

Later, Lucy and I helped Aunt Polly water the new garden she had put in with her neighbor. The yard was always gorgeous, the cottage garden on the side of the house in full bloom. The new garden was an attempt to grow strawberries, my favorite. I kneeled to inspect the small sprouts coming through when I heard a deep male voice call out.

"Hey ya, Polly!"

I looked up to find a man walking up the driveway, and I had to blink. Oh, shit, this delicious looking guy had to be the neighbor. My hot pocket got a little hotter. Holy hell.

He was at least six feet, built larger, like a football player, not fat but not ripped. His arms were big and stretched the material of the T-shirt he was wearing, and those arms were completely sleeved in tattoos.

Fuck me.

And to top off the tattoos, he had a beard. Not a patchy, shitty beard. A full, 'I want to pull it' beard. He was everything I liked in a man, which was not good because I had terrible taste in men.

His sandy brown hair was thick and wavy, shaved close on the sides and longer and messy on top. I wondered if that hair cut had a name like the 'pull my hair while I bang you' cut.

His steel gray eyes found mine, and he smiled. I melted a little more before I pulled myself together and stood up. I couldn't let him see my weakness for the whole big, bad boy package he had going on.

"You must be Evan," he said, walking over to me and holding out his hand. I took it and shook, noticing how large it was compared to mine.

"I am," I said as sweetly as I could. I wanted to growl at him and tell him to go away, but Aunt Polly liked this guy so I couldn't. I needed the visions of him fucking me to go away. "And you are?"

"I'm Levi Kincaid, her neighbor. Well, neighbor and friend," he clarified.

Aunt Polly came over to him, and he put his big arm around her.

"How are you today, Polly? You dressed to work, or what?" he teased.

Aunt Polly smiled. "I am! I wanted to show Evan around the new garden, and I was hoping you two would see each other. I thought you could take my niece out on a date."

My eyes went wide. She may have been having a good day, but her mouth seemed to not be.

"Oh, Aunt Polly," I stuttered. " I don't need to be taken out on a date. I'm here to help you."

Levi laughed. "If you girls need anything I'm across the road."

"Thanks, Levi. I gave Evan your number along with Rex's," Lucy told him.

Levi looked at me and smiled. "I'm available any time of day, especially when it comes to Polly."

"I appreciate it," I said, not making eye contact.

"Okay, then. I just wanted to come say hi and introduce myself to the niece I've heard so much about. It was nice meeting you, Evan."

I forced an awkward smile. "You, too."

He hugged Aunt Polly and waved to Lucy as he walked down the driveway to cross the road back to his house.

15

Watching him walk away was just as nice as watching him walk towards me.

Aunt Polly laughed.

"What's so funny?" I asked her, annoyed because I already knew what she was going to say.

"You like him," she accused, her smile mischievous.

"I just met him," I defended myself, even though she was right. I liked what I saw. A lot. But, I wasn't here for that. I had too many bad experiences with men, trying to find one I wanted to be with. So many men, in fact, that a lot of the women in the town I had lived in liked to call me nicknames like slut and whore. Maybe I was a slut, but I wasn't a whore.

"I may be old and senile, but I still know those looks the two of you were giving each other. He likes you, too."

Oh, brother.

"Aunt Polly, you better not have wanted me here to set me up with your neighbor," I told her, a smile playing on my lips.

"No dear, but if you do end up dating him, I wouldn't be upset. He is such a good boy," she said, walking back towards the house.

Good boy my ass. Levi screamed bad in so many ways.

CHAPTER THREE

LEVI

Fuck me, man. Evan was gorgeous. I had watched her drive in the night before, her black car pulling in and her getting out of it. I watched as Polly hugged her and as they walked up the front steps. I decided I would wait until the next day to go over and check Evan out closer. Polly had been excited Evan was coming, and I wanted to give them the time alone.

So, I sat on my porch, in the dark, drinking a few beers and watching the house across the road from me. The house of a woman I had adopted as a mother, a woman who I had dropped everything to help, a woman who had shared with me family secrets she would take to the grave. A woman I had shared some of my secrets with, as well. As bad as it sounds, I didn't think she was in the frame of mind the day I told her that she would remember. But, it felt good to tell someone things I couldn't tell many other people. I loved Polly; she was one amazing lady.

Over the years, she had spoken of Evan often. Telling me about their summers together, and showing me pictures of Evan as a young girl. The woman she grew up to be made my dick twitch. She was stunning, and that was not a term I ever used. Sure, I had said a chick was hot, or beautiful, but not stunning. Evan was just that. Stunning.

When I walked over earlier that day, I had been watching her the entire time. She was inspecting the strawberry garden Polly and I had planted, and I was inspecting her ass.

I wanted her.

The sun was shining on her caramel-colored hair, bringing out the blonde streaks. The kind of streaks you didn't buy at a salon, natural ones caused by the sun. Evan's eyes were a hazel color, not green but not brown, with flecks of gold in them, and they were framed by the longest, black eyelashes I had ever seen. Her dark eyebrows set those gorgeous eyes off, and I was intrigued. Her skin was tan, but she didn't seem like the kind of woman who would lay in a tanning bed. Polly had darker skin, a family trait?

Evan was taller, about five eight, and her curves were proportionate. Bigger tits with a small waist, round hips, and a bouncy bubble ass. Perfect.

I yelled out to Polly, getting all three women's attention as I walked up the driveway. Lucy and Polly waved to me, Evan just watched me.

"You must be Evan," I said as I put my hand out for her to shake it. She placed her small hand in mine.

"And you are?" she asked.

I introduced myself as Polly's neighbor, even though I counted Polly as family.

I spoke with Polly for a few minutes before she decided to announce I should take Evan on a date. I smiled and shook my head as Evan seemed to stutter over Polly's outburst. I had to hand it to Evan. She dodged it smoothly, saying she didn't need to be taken on a date, even though I had no problem with the idea.

I decided it was time to let the ladies do whatever it was they were doing and be on my way.

"If you girls need anything, I'm across the road," I told them, not hiding my laughter. Polly was a firecracker.

Lucy, Polly's home nurse, let me know she had given Evan my number if she needed my help. I turned to Evan and let her know I was available any time of day when it came to Polly. And I was.

After saying good-bye, I walked back over to my place and saw the dark, cherry-red Nova parked in my driveway. That particular piece of shit belonged to my closest friend and somewhat brother, Rex. I was pretty sure he had a home of his own, but somehow he was never there.

I walked up my front porch and walked in, letting the screen door slam behind me.

"You better not be eating all my fucking food, asshole!" I called out.

Walking into my kitchen, I found him just as I had pictured him, face in my fridge and a beer in his hand. A beer he didn't bring over.

"I'm not eating all of it," he said, standing up to look at me.

"What's her name?" I asked, motioning to the black eye he was sporting.

"Huh?"

"The black eye, dipshit. Who gave it to you?"

"Oh, that. It wasn't a she," he said, shutting the refrigerator door empty-handed. "It was her husband."

I laughed. "Rex, dude, I've told you before, you got to stop fucking married women."

He took a long pull from his beer. "Man, the married chicks seem to be the hottest and horniest ones around."

He had a point.

"Where were you?" Rex asked. "Over at Polly's?"

"Yep. Her niece got here last night," I told him. I opened the fridge and grabbed myself a beer and then walked out to the front porch. Rex followed.

"So? Is she as hot as the pictures Polly's shown us?"

"Yeah, she is pretty fucking hot," I confirmed.

"Dang, fresh meat." Rex wagged his eyebrows at me.

"Oh no. No fucking way. You keep your dirty fucking hands off her, got me?" I growled. I was not letting that dirtbag touch Polly's pride and joy. I loved Rex, but he was a fucking low life who used and abused women.

"Hey man, I wasn't talking about me," he said, pointing at me. "You, my friend, need to get laid. The chicks in this town don't want anything to do with you, so maybe you'd have better luck with the new girl."

"No, I don't touch the girls in this town because your dick has touched every single one of them." I laughed.

"Lies," Rex said as he pointed down the road towards the small town we called home. "There's a few chicks at the market I haven't touched."

"The market? You mean the sixty-year-old church ladies who work there? Your restraint is that of a fucking saint."

Rex thought for a second. "I don't know. That Delores who runs checkstand three looks like she would be a wild one in bed, and I'm pretty sure she wears dentures. She could gum my dick like there's no tomorrow."

"You're fucking sick."

Both of us laughed.

I met Rex when I was eighteen. I had moved to Kendrick to go to work with my uncle at his excavating company after doing some time in juvenile hall. Rex and I worked as laborers together, clicking from day one. At the time, we were both delinquents, Rex more so than me. I was ready to pull my life back together, but Rex? Not so much. He still partied, drank and smoked too much weed while I stayed in at night. I was on probation, so I lived with my aunt and uncle, one of the terms. My probation officer dropped in a few times to check on me, but after a while, the visits stopped. I thought my uncle had something to do with it, but I never found out. Either way, my five-year probation went by smoothly.

My uncle died of a heart attack a few years later, leaving the company to me. My aunt didn't mind; he left everything else to her. She sold their home and moved to Florida, and I hadn't heard from her since. Good riddance, she was a bitch.

Rex and I had been running the company smoothly ever since, becoming active members of our community. Hell, even the town sheriff liked us. We sponsored little league, donated to the booster clubs, attended charities—all the sort of shit that made us liked by the people who mattered. It was the shit that made the people who mattered overlook Rex's womanizing, drinking, and drug using. The sort of shit that made the people who mattered overlook my past.

Sheriff Brendan Cash had been the deputy on duty the night I was arrested nineteen years ago. Brendan was the one who put in the good word for me to the judge who saw my case. He was the one who got my time lowered to only three years. And, Brenden was the one who suggested I be released to my uncle when I got out. Why? Because I was released to my uncle who lived in Kendrick, the town Deputy Cash was now the sheriff of.

I heard my cell phone ringing in the house. I jumped up from where Rex and I had been sitting on my porch drinking a couple beers and went inside to grab it. Looking at the number on the screen, I saw it was Polly.

"Hey Polly," I answered, "what's going on?"

"Oh, nothing. I just saw that Rex was over there, and I wanted to invite you boys over for supper," she said. Polly had us over often to eat; she might have been the reason my stomach was a little flabbier than it should be.

"We'll be there. How soon?" I asked.

"As soon as you see the pizza delivery boy drive up, come on over." She laughed.

"We'll bring some beer," I told her.

Fifteen minutes later, Rex and I were walking up the front porch of Polly's house, not knocking as we walked in. We never knocked, but it took Evan by surprise.

"Holy shit!" she yelled. "You can't scare me like that!"

"Sorry," I said, laughing at her.

"Come on; we're sitting out back," she motioned for us to follow her, but not before I caught her doing a once over on me.

We followed, and I watched Rex as his eyes never left Evan's round ass. I punched his arm, getting his attention.

"Don't fucking try it," I warned him.

"Hey, brother, she's all yours."

All mine sounded pretty fucking good.

CHAPTER FOUR

EVAN

Levi and his friend Rex came out to the back porch to join Aunt Polly, Lucy and I for some greasy, delicious pizza, and wouldn't you know it? They brought the beer.

Levi saw me eyeing the green bottles and offered me one.

"Thank you," I said as he opened it for me.

"No problem. Evan, this is Rex. Rex, this is Evan," Levi made the introductions as if he didn't want to.

I smiled at the tall man. "Nice to meet you, Rex."

"Likewise," he replied, a smirk on his lips.

Rex was that kind of guy women fantasized about, but didn't want to admit it. His ink-dark hair was to his shoulders and looked as if it hadn't been washed in days. The kind of hair that had those beach waves women would kill for. His full, dark beard was a bit on the long side, not groomed like Levi's was. Rex had piercing blue eyes framed by the darkest lashes I had ever seen on a man. He was taller than Levi, but not much, and his build was more on the trim side. He was muscular, though, and heavily tattooed from his neck down except for the tattoo above his brow that read 'saved' and the bull ring through his nose. I noticed even his hands were tattooed with what looked like playing cards. I now understood why Lucy had said he didn't look friendly, but the look Rex was giving me at that moment was more than friendly. He was fucking me with his eyes, and I was blushing like a teenage girl.

Rex was a dirty fucking fantasy.

I looked away from his sex stare and concentrated all my attention on my pizza.

"So, Evan," I heard Rex start. "Polly here told us you're a teacher? Is that right?"

I looked up. Rex and Levi were both watching me while Aunt Polly and Lucy seemed oblivious to the tension that was on that back porch.

I smiled. "Uh, yeah. I am."

Levi leaned in, putting his elbows on the table.

"What do you teach?" he asked.

"I teach middle school, mostly English. I thought middle school kids would be easier to teach, but they are ruthless and master manipulators," I laughed.

"Are you going to try to get a teaching job here?" Levi asked, his eyes trained on me. The man was intense.

"Yeah," I stammered. "I think I'm going to apply down at the school. It'll give me the summer to get settled in and get Polly's daily routines down."

Levi smiled at me. "Well, like I said before, I can help out."

"So," I started, wanting to get the subject off me, "what is it that you do?"

The question was aimed at both men. I had wondered what type of job these two could possibly work. Office jobs were definitely out.

"I own a small excavating company, and Rex here helps me run it," Levi informed me.

I could see that. They both looked like they would work outdoors doing some sort of manly job.

"There's a lot of business for that?" I asked.

"Oh yeah, we do commercial and private."

I looked over to Rex who was still ogling me, or maybe that was just his normal look? I smiled at him and put my attention back on Levi.

"Well, the garden you put in here turned out nice."

"Thanks," Levi said. "Polly wanted a strawberry garden, so she got one."

I watched as Levi looked at Polly who was not part of the conversation at all. He smiled at her and patted her hand, getting her attention. She looked at him and smiled back.

"Louis, you know how pizza gives you heartburn," she said, and the mood at the table changed.

She hadn't been here with us, after all.

*

After we cleaned up from our delivered dinner, Rex and Levi said goodnight, both kissing Aunt Polly on the cheek and hugging Lucy before they left. When they came to me, both stopped, and I didn't know what to do. I looked at Levi, and he smiled.

"Night, Evan. I'm sure I'll see you soon."

"Goodnight," I murmured, and he walked out the front door. I turned and found Rex standing right in my comfort bubble, and the next thing I knew, he engulfed me in a giant hug.

"I can do this because I feel like I already know you," he said.

I patted his back as he held me, feeling extremely awkward when he pulled away and walked out. I watched as Rex caught up to a waiting Levi, who then smacked the back of his head.

"I got a hug from her!" Rex bragged, which made me laugh.

"Yeah, I saw. Real smooth fucker," I heard Levi respond as they walked away.

Having these two around was going to be tricky. I kept telling myself I couldn't fuck either of them because it would complicate the shit out of my life in Kendrick, but, it wouldn't be the first time my vagina did all the thinking for me.

CHAPTER FIVE

EVAN

The next few days went smoothly. Lucy came over early in the morning and stayed until after dinner, helping me with Aunt Polly. My aunt had been in good spirits, and there were only a few times where she was confused. The one thing she was never unsure of was who I was. She never mistook me for someone else or forgot my name. I was a constant for her.

The days were warm, and we passed our time tending to gardens and playing card games on the back porch. Lucy was an angel sent straight from heaven, that I was sure of. She never lost her patience with Aunt Polly, or me for that matter.

"Evan—" Lucy smiled at me. "Why don't you get out of the house for a bit. Polly is napping in her recliner; we're good here for about an hour."

"Are you sure?" I asked.

"Yes."

*

I walked out behind the house and made my way to the back of the property. I used to know every square inch of that place. I walked through the light cover of trees that could almost pass for a forest, finding the creek that traveled to the large sycamore tree at the back of the property. The creek had been part of many summer adventures for me, and I found the section that widened and deepened to a small swimming hole. Aunt Polly and I had nicknamed it the "criver" because it was too wide to be a creek and too narrow to be a river. We used to come out here and swim almost all day, packing picnics of peanut butter and jelly sandwiches and old fashioned potato chips. I wondered if I could bring her out once summer started. It was going on my to-do list.

I took my shoes off and dipped my toes into the water, which was still a bit on the chilly side. Looking off into the distance, I could see the old sycamore tree standing tall and proud, a reminder that it knew my secrets.

Sitting along the bank of the creek I laid back, stretching my arms above my head and watching the clouds float by. I wasn't sure how long I was there before I closed my eyes and began to drift off, just like when I was a kid.

The days at Aunt Polly's hadn't been as awful as I thought they would be with her new husband there. He worked during the day, so it was just us girls. We still made our favorite peanut butter and jelly sandwiches and packed them to take down to the criver to swim, and we still picked the wildflowers that grew near the sycamore tree to make flower crowns. Aunt Polly seemed happy, so I decided I would be happy for her.

The only days Louis was around was on the weekends, unless he got called out to do sheriff stuff. I wanted him to get called away. He tried to butt in and be part of the things my aunt and I always did, and unfortunately, my aunt would let him. I tried to like Louis, but I couldn't. He grossed me out, and, even though I was only twelve, I still knew what people did behind closed doors and to think of my aunt letting that guy do that stuff to her made me want to barf.

On a Saturday afternoon, a few weeks after the wedding, I decided to go down to my favorite tree and read the copy of 'Flowers in the Attic' I had checked out at the library. All my friends back home had read it, but my mom wouldn't let me. So, I decided this was going to be the summer I read all of V.C. Andrews' books.

I walked out along the creek, picking flowers and putting them in my hair, which I had decided I wouldn't brush all summer. I wanted to look like the hippie girls I had seen pictures of in a copy of 'Time' magazine. Aunt Polly had some old broomstick skirts, and she let me have them. They fit perfectly, and I paired them with the old Harley Davidson tank tops I had of my mom's. They fit me tight; my boobs had come in way earlier than my friends, and I hated it. But, looking at all the women in my family, I should have known. My mom was a D cup, and I was sure my aunt was, also. I was already in a B cup.

As I approached the tree, I saw the rope swing Louis had hung. This wasn't my first trip to the tree since I had arrived, but I hadn't used the stupid swing. Why did that guy think he could touch my tree?

The swing was a single rope with a flat piece of wood with a hole drilled through it at the end held on by a thick knot. Looking up to the branch it was tied to, I wondered how he got up there. No way he could have climbed.

I walked over to swing and tugged, testing it. Looking around, I didn't see anyone, so I put my book into the front of my tank top and placed one leg over the piece of wood. Pushing off with my foot, I threw my other leg over and began to swing. I leaned back and watched as the branches and leaves swirled by, the sun playing peek-a-boo through them. I would never admit it to anyone, but the swing may not have been a bad thing. I slowed down and pulled out my book. Wrapping my arms around the rope, I began to read.

I had to have been there for at least an hour when the light swinging motion I had maintained stopped. Looking behind me, I found Louis. I hadn't even heard him approach.

"What are you reading?" he asked as he smiled at me.

"Just a book from the library," I answered, trying to move away from him. He didn't seem to understand personal space.

"Oh yeah? What's it about?"

"Siblings locked in an attic."

"Hm, that doesn't sound like a book a little girl would want to read," Louis replied.

"Well, I'm twelve, so I don't classify as a little girl anymore," I told him, trying to go back to my reading and not notice how close he was standing.

"No, you sure don't," he said, his voice changing to something I didn't like.

I tried to ignore him and act as if him being in my space wasn't bothering me, but it was. He knew it; I could tell. He leaned in closer, reading over my shoulder. I stiffened as I felt something hard and blunt poke into the middle of my back. I knew what it was, and I felt as he rubbed himself back and forth. I didn't know what to do. I couldn't get off the swing; he was still holding it. I tried to think fast.

"I need to get back to the house. I promised Aunt Polly I would help her get the green beans ready for dinner," I stuttered as I wriggled out of his hold. He let go of the ropes, and I jumped off. I turned to face him and immediately noticed the bulge in his pants, and I wished I hadn't looked at him. He walked closer to me, tucking a piece of my hair behind my ear. I stared at him, frozen. He smiled at me, and I turned and walked as fast as I could until I knew he couldn't see me anymore. Once he was out of sight, I sprinted as fast as I could to the safety of my aunt.

CHAPTER SIX

LEVI

I had gone over to Polly's to check in on her, and Lucy told me she was napping. Polly loved her sleep, and I was envious.

"Evan walked to the back of the property. She's been gone awhile," Lucy told me, smiling.

"Oh yeah? I could go check on her," I offered.

"Maybe you should," she replied with a wink.

I walked along the creek knowing it was the trail Evan would take. Polly and I had taken many evening strolls after dinner together following the same path. The property had been Polly's for years, and she'd had plenty of offers to buy it. She turned down every single one, basically telling developers to fuck off. I wasn't sure how, but Polly had money. She never said so, but she didn't work, and she didn't seem to hurt for funds. Having an in-home nurse wasn't cheap. Lucy lived there five days a week, and there was a part-time weekend nurse for the other two days. Polly had mentioned an inheritance once, but I never pressed the subject.

I saw Evan laying back on the bank of the creek where it widened enough to make a swimming hole. Over the summers, I had ventured out there enough times after a long day of work to cool off. As I approached, I saw she had her eyes closed with her arms stretched above her head. Fuck, she was gorgeous. She was in a pair of faded jeans that rode low on her hips, a white T-shirt, and flip flops. Her hair was piled on top of her head and was a mess, but she looked beautiful. Natural. It was something I didn't see enough of from women. Most were overdone to appear younger, only making themselves look haggard and desperate. Evan looked neither of those things.

I stood over her, blocking the sun from her until she opened her eyes and jumped.

"Holy mother fuck!" she yelled as she sat up, making me laugh.

"You kiss your mother with that mouth?" I asked, taking a seat next to her.

She chuckled. "Hardly, that would mean my mother would have to see me for me to kiss her."

"Ah, mom not around? I get that."

Evan was quiet for a minute, and I watched her out the corner of my eye. She seemed lost in thought, her long lashes fluttering now and then and her chest rising and falling in a steady movement.

"So, Levi," she said, breaking the silence, "tell me about yourself."

"Not much to tell," I lied.

"Ever been married?"

"Fuck, no."

She laughed. "Against marriage?"

"No, not against it. People can get married as much as they want. I just haven't wanted to."

"Same," she confessed. "I went out with this guy once, and the first thing he asked me was if I had kids. I thought that was crazy, but he said most women my age in the dating scene were divorced, single moms."

"He's probably right," I told her. "I have dated my fair share of single moms. They need to have a life, too."

Evan nodded. "Yeah, they do. But the way he made it sound was that there must be something wrong with me because I wasn't a divorced, single mom, you know?"

"No, I don't know." I looked at her. "There is nothing wrong with you just because you haven't had a failed marriage."

"You don't even know me. You can't make that assumption," Evan said, her eyes boring into mine.

"I know enough," was all I said. She narrowed her eyes at me. "Polly loves to tell me about you," I confessed.

"I'm sure she does."

"She thinks you hung the moon, you know."

"And here I thought she did." Evan laughed, the sound light and musical.

Evan and I sat on the bank of the creek talking for a little while longer. I told her how Rex and I became friends, leaving out the juvenile hall portion, and she told me about spending summers in Kendrick. To her, this place was home. It made me wonder about her relationship with her parents.

"Oh, my dad was never in the picture, and my mom was a nurse. She worked the night shift, so I was with babysitters a lot. That's how I ended up spending my summers here. Polly insisted. Don't get me wrong, my mom tried her hardest, but she was just never around because of work. I never went without, and when mom was home, we had so much fun together. She was a young mom, so she tried a little too hard to be my friend, but that's who introduced me to reading. Mom loved to read; it's actually how I got my name."

"You're named after a book?" I asked.

"Kind of. My mom was into romance novels when she was pregnant with me. One of her favorites had a prince named Evan in it, and she was sure I was going to be a boy. She didn't find out while she was pregnant, so when I was born not a boy, it was decided it's now a girl's name."

"Evan fits you," I told her, and it did.

"Maybe, but growing up I wished I was a Jessica or an Ashley because all the popular girls were named Jessica and Ashley. I thought if I was named one of those I would be popular, too."

"You weren't popular?"

"Not at all," she said.

"Me either."

"Really? You look like you would have been," Evan stated.

"Really, I was the smelly kid. You know? The one who's mom and step-dad smoked and drank in the house? The kid who was dirty and wore clothes a little too small for him? I was that kid."

"Oh," was all she said.

36

"Hey, don't feel sorry for me. It all worked out. My uncle took me in, and my life has been peachy ever since."

"Your uncle, huh?" she started. "You know, Levi? It seems you and I have more in common than I thought."

Turning, I looked at her, staring into those hazel eyes that were more green than anything at that moment.

"More than you know, Evan."

CHAPTER SEVEN

EVAN

Levi and Rex became semi-permanent fixtures around the house and the property. One or the other would come by late in the day to check on us, making sure we didn't need any help. You know, manly shit that us helpless little ladies couldn't do on our own. Honestly, I didn't mind. I was as far from a feminist as could be. I didn't mind a strong hand willing to help with the heavy stuff. The two gruff looking men were starting to grow on me, and I was beginning to understand why Polly thought so highly of them. They were thoughtful and kind, and from the outer appearance of them both, most wouldn't expect it.

Rex wasn't around as often as Levi, and when I asked about him, Levi would tell me he was out "most likely committing some sort of crime."

I wondered if he was joking.

Weeks had passed since I arrived, and Aunt Polly, Lucy and I had fallen into a fantastic routine. The days had gone by quickly. Although Aunt Polly was doing well, she still had her bad days. I was able to handle them much easier than the first few days after I got there. It broke my heart to look at her and see her eyes unfocused, the tell-tale sign she was having a slip of her memory. She was so confused and sometimes scared, and then she would get mean. Lucy told me that was normal, but it didn't mean I needed to be okay with it.

Polly hated it when she thought I was talking down to her, at one point telling me I was being a selfish little brat.

"Did you forget everything I've done for you?" she hissed, pointing her finger at me. "I gave up my entire life for you, so don't you act high and mighty with me, little girl."

The outburst stemmed from explaining to her that 'Roseanne' was no longer on TV.

Some days, I wondered if I had made the right decision to come to take care of my aunt. There was more than one night I found myself silently crying after a day of constant reminding and explaining. She was getting worse, and I knew it. I hated seeing her slip away from me.

"Evan?" I heard Levi call my name followed by the slam of the screen door. It was early evening on a Sunday night, and I had just gotten Aunt Polly into her nightgown and her hair brushed.

"We're coming downstairs," I called out to him as I walked behind my aunt. I put my hand on her shoulder only to have her shrug me off.

"I can do it myself!"

I backed off, and as I walked down, my eyes met Levi's. His face was full of concern.

"Hey there, Polly." He smiled as she came to the last step, offering his hand to her.

Reaching her hand out to him she laughed. "Well, aren't you a handsome one?"

Levi looked at me, and I shook my head, letting him know it hadn't been the best day. He looked back to Polly and pasted a tight, fake smile on his face.

"Come on, let's get you comfortable," he said as he led her to her recliner. She didn't argue as they walked into the living room. Once she was situated with the remote, Levi came to where I leaned against the living room entry.

"Bad day?" he asked.

"You could say that."

"You're doing fine. You know that, right?"

"The only thing I feel like I am doing right is that she still knows who I am, but that might not last. This is fucking hard," I sighed. "Aunt Polly," I shouted, "I'm going to sit out on the porch. Holler if you need anything, okay?"

"That's fine, dear," she called back.

I motioned for Levi to follow me, and we walked out into the warm evening air. I sat on the porch swing, and he took the seat next to me. My body was hyper-aware of his closeness. Neither of us spoke for a few minutes; we just rocked the swing back and forth.

"I came over here to let you know I have to go out of town for a couple days for work," Levi said, breaking our silence. "I should be back by Wednesday."

"Rex going with you?"

"Yeah, it's a big job. I need him. I'm hoping he sobers up enough by tomorrow morning."

"What?" I asked.

Levi laughed. "Oh yeah, he's been on a fucking bender all weekend. Met some chick named Gretchen and all they have done is drink, fuck and get high for the last two days. He just dragged his ass to my house an hour ago and is sleeping it off on my couch."

"Wow." I didn't know what else to say.

"Yeah, wow is right. But, he'll be ready to go tomorrow. He always is. I don't get it," Levi chuckled.

"Get what?"

"I don't get how he can fuck off like that for days at a time and then wake up and be fine. I get drunk, and it takes me a full day to recover."

I laugh. "Maybe he's just more practiced than you."

"You're probably right." Levi laughed, and we talked a little while longer before he said goodnight and that he would see us soon. I watched him walk down the driveway and across the street to his house. I was going to miss his daily check-ins and looked forward to him coming back to Kendrick.

*

I thought about Levi while he was gone, some of our conversations to be exact. He was an interesting guy. At first glance, he was intimidating and hard looking, a guy some people might be leery of, including myself. But, over the weeks I had gotten to know him, I realized there was so much more to him. Levi Kincaid was a man I needed to be careful around. Why? Because I could see myself easily falling for him, and if

I wanted to be perfectly honest with myself, the fall had already started.

On Wednesday afternoon, Aunt Polly and I sat out back together. Her crocheting while I read a seedy romance novel. It had been a good day; she was bright-eyed and happy, humming while she made washcloths.

The day was warm and humid, a preview of the summer that was right around the corner. I lounged in an Adirondack chair in a pair of cut off jean shorts and an old plaid shirt with the sleeves rolled to the elbow. I felt very Daisy Duke, but the shirt was one of my favorites. You know the kind—old and worn in, the one you probably should have donated to a charity store a long time ago but you can't part with it.

I rubbed my bare feet over the soft grass as I read my sexy book, taking my time on the dirty parts. It had been quite some time since I had a man touch me, so if the only way I was getting my happy time was through reading, so be it. Thank goodness for my imagination; it came in handy on my nightly dates with my trusty battery-powered rabbit. It was tucked away in my nightstand, but lately, I had been having a lot of one on one time with it. That wasn't because of the books, or maybe it was the books and Levi. I thought about him when bringing myself to orgasm. What it would feel like to have his hands on me, his mouth between my legs, his cock buried deep inside of me. I reminded myself every night after I had come that all I could have was the fantasy. Not to let myself get involved with him. Being the one to ruin his relationship with Aunt Polly would hurt her, and I was good at ruining relationships. Levi had to be off limits.

"Oh shoot," Aunt Polly cried as she suddenly stood up, her crocheting falling to the ground.

I went over to her, taking her by the elbow to help steady her.

"What's wrong?" I asked.

"I need to make Louis his dinner! He likes it to be ready when he gets home, and I haven't started it."

"It's okay, Aunt Polly. I can get dinner started," I told her as I bent over, picking up her washcloths. I stood up and handed them back to her. She snatched them out of my hands and huffed.

"I don't need you making my husband dinner," she spat as she glared at me. I held up my hands, letting her know I didn't mean to upset her.

"Okay, Aunt Polly. I just wanted to help you," I said.

Her face softened, and tears came to her eyes.

"Oh, sweetheart, I am so sorry. Sometimes, things just slip by me, and I can't remember," she said, the tears sliding down her face.

I took her hands in mine and smiled at her.

"It's okay. I could never be upset with you. We're in this together," I reassured her.

"You're a good girl, Evan. You always have been."

The compliment made me want to tear up as well, but I held back. I just nodded at her and helped her back into her chair. She resumed her crocheting, and I went back to my book, although I couldn't get back into the story. All I could think about was if I was enough to take care of her alone.

*

Aunt Polly had fallen asleep in her recliner after we came inside. I turned down the volume on the TV while she napped and made my way into the kitchen to get something started for dinner. As I was grabbing some potatoes out of the pantry, I heard the front screen door slam shut, and the familiar sound of boots thudding down the hall.

"Evan?" I heard Levi call out.

"In the kitchen!" I checked my appearance in the reflection of the kitchen window, smoothing down a few stray hairs. I saw Levi come in behind me, and I turned around, meeting the steel gray stare of a man who I couldn't stop thinking about.

"Hey," I said, my voice breathy and deep. *What the fuck was that all about?*

"Hey."

"How was your trip?" I asked, turning back around to the sink and busying myself with washing the potatoes. I heard Levi approach. Checking the reflection in the window, I saw he was standing behind me, looking me up and down. There was a flutter in my lower stomach, the one you get when you see someone who makes you feel. That flutter of a million butterflies trying to burst free.

Levi came and stood next to me, leaning back against the counter, his arms crossed in front of him.

"It was good. How were things here? Did I miss anything exciting?"

The question made me laugh. I turned around and mimicked his stance.

"Exciting? Yes. You missed so much excitement while you were gone," I teased. "So much."

"How is Polly?" Levi asked, and the concern in his voice made my stomach flutter again. He cared so much for my aunt.

I shook my head. "Some days are okay, but not great. Today, she snapped at me and then realized she had and apologized."

Levi was quiet for a moment, his stare directed to the floor. Looking up, his eyes found mine, and he smiled a crooked smirk.

"You're still doing just fine," he reassured me. I needed to hear that and coming from him meant so much more than from anyone else. Levi was important to my aunt, and he was quickly becoming important to me.

"Thank you," I told him, giving him a warm smile. Levi calmed me, made me feel like everything would be okay when he was around. No one, besides Aunt Polly, had ever done that for me. I felt myself falling a little more every time Levi spoke those quiet and sweet words he always seemed to find at just the right time. A guy like Levi could swoop in and steal a girls heart without her ever seeing it coming, and right at that moment, I was completely blinded.

CHAPTER EIGHT

LEVI

Evan needed a night out. A night for herself. A date, just like Polly wanted when she first arrived in Kendrick, and that was exactly what I was going to do.

Picking up my cell, I hit the call button for the number to the one person I knew would be able to sit with Polly while I took Evan out.

"Hello?"

"Hey there, Lucy. How are you?", I asked, trying to make my voice as friendly as possible.

"I'm good. Is everything okay?" I could hear the alarm in her voice.

"Yeah, everything is fine. I was just wondering if I could sweet talk you into hanging out with Polly tonight?"

I heard some shuffling on the other end and a door slam. Looking out the window, I could make out Lucy standing on the front porch of Polly's house.

"I could, but why?"

"Because I want to take Evan out. You know, get her out of the house for a few hours," I told her.

"That sounds like a great idea, Levi. What time?" Lucy asked.

"How about now?" The sun was setting, and we weren't going anywhere fancy. I wanted to take Evan to get a beer, and she didn't need to get dressed up for that.

"Does Evan know you're coming?"

"Nope, I'm just coming over and stealing her," I joked.

I fired up my classic Chevy Silverado, letting it idle for a minute while I locked up my house. I loved that truck; it wasn't beautiful, but it was built, and it was one of my most prized possessions.

Jumping in, I drove across the road and down the drive to Polly's house. I watched as Evan came out onto the front porch, and confusion was written on her gorgeous face. I never drove over.

Stopping in front of the porch, I leaned out the window as Lucy came out to join Evan on the porch, a wide smile across her face.

"Get in, loser," I called out.

"Did you just quote 'Mean Girls'?" Evan asked.

"What?" I asked, even though that was exactly what I was quoting. Rex and I watched that movie a lot; Lindsey Lohan's tits were fantastic in it.

"What are you doing, Levi?" Evan questioned, her look suspicious.

"It's okay, honey. Go! Levi already checked with me, and Polly will be fine. You need a minute to yourself," Lucy coaxed, smiling at her.

Evan looked back to me, and I waved at her to get in the truck. For a faint second, a flicker of something shone in

47

her eyes, and if I wasn't mistaken, it was the look of freedom and lust. She went back inside and came out a few minutes later, her messy bun not quite as messy and a pair of flip flops on her feet. She looked fucking hot as sin in the cut-offs and old plaid shirt she had unbuttoned just enough to see the right amount of cleavage. I would have loved to see everything that old shirt was hiding, but for now, the peep show I was getting would be enough.

Evan opened the passenger door and climbed in, shutting it and rolling down the window.

"I won't be late, Lucy!"

"Take your time. We'll be just fine. See you when you get home," Lucy called out as I put the truck in reverse and backed up. Looking over to Evan, I smiled.

"You want to get a beer and the best cheesesteaks in town?" I asked her as I gunned it down the driveway.

"Oh, fuck yeah. That sounds like heaven," she replied, her eyes dancing as she smiled back at me. I loved the way she spoke, no filter or inhibitions. Just Evan and that mouth like a sailor.

We pulled into the back parking lot of Andy's and went in. The usual crowd was there, including Rex. As soon as he saw me with Evan, his mouth spread into the biggest shit-eating grin I had ever seen. He was sitting at a table with a bunch of the local bikers, some I knew to be good guys. The others I knew to be drug dealers. All of them friends with Rex.

He stood up and came over to us, grabbing Evan into a bear hug, continuing to smile at me. I flipped him off. He blew me a kiss.

"What are you two doing here?" he asked as he let Evan go. She turned to me and gave an awkward smile, her cheeks flushed. Was she blushing?

"Same thing as you," I told him, turning to walk to the bar, Evan and Rex following behind.

"You came to buy some coke and get laid?" Rex asked, looking at Evan with wide, questioning eyes as we stood at the bar. She looked at me and back to Rex, who was still looking at her waiting for her to answer.

"Um, I don't think we came to do the exact same thing as you. We just wanted a beer and some food," she said.

"Oh," Rex said, a look of disappointment on his smug fucking face.

The three of us sat at a table in the corner drinking our beers and eating the cheesesteaks I'd ordered. Most women are self-conscious when they eat, but not Evan. She devoured the greasy sandwich, licking her fingers when she was done. And yes, I watched her lick them imagining her licking my dick the exact same way, complete with smacking sounds. I noticed Rex watching her the same way I was, so I kicked him under the table. He smiled at me, shook his head, and got up. He went over to one of the bikers I knew to be one of his drug dealers and sat down.

"You want another beer?" I asked Evan.

"Sure," she replied, smiling.

It took the bartender a few minutes to get our beers. Once they were in my hands, I turned to go back to the table and stopped. There was a guy sitting across from Evan. I could tell by the fake smile on her face that Evan didn't know him. He was hitting on her. Hadn't the asshole just seen me sitting there? As I approached, I recognized him. His name was Dylan, and he was well known around the area to be a fan of getting girls plastered and taking them home.

I sat down next to Evan, handing her beer to her as I stared Dylan down.

"Oh, hey there, Levi," Dylan said. I could hear the nervousness in his voice.

"Dylan." I nodded to him as I took a pull off my beer. "I see you met my girl, Evan. She lives across the street from me." I was letting him know I had eyes on her.

Dylan smiled at me. "It's good to know your neighbors," he said. "Nice to meet you, Evan." And with that, the puke got up and left the table.

Evan didn't ask anything about my behavior with Dylan, either that or she didn't realize I was pissing on my territory. We sat for a while longer, talking and laughing, and watching Rex make a fool of himself dancing with some of the town girls. Dylan sat in the opposite corner with his friends, and I caught him glancing our way a time or two.

After about an hour, I saw him get up to use the men's room, so I excused myself and followed him in. Just my luck, no one else was in there. He stood at the urinal and didn't notice me at first, but when he zipped his fly and turned around, I made damn sure he noticed me.

"You will stay the fuck away from Evan, we clear?" I snarled, not touching him.

"Yeah, man. We're clear," he stuttered. I never liked the guy. I had heard too many rumors about him liking his girls passed out drunk.

"Great, because if I hear of you trying to get her drunk so you can fuck her while she's passed out, I will fucking end you," I said, my voice low. I patted him on the shoulder and turned around, storming out of the bathroom.

Right then and there, I knew that sooner or later I would claim Evan.

CHAPTER NINE

EVAN

"I had a great time," I told Levi as we drove back to my aunt's house. "And those cheesesteaks were so good."

"We'll do it again," he said. He looked sexy driving his old truck down the dark country road. It took everything I had not to stare at him.

"I'd like that."

He pulled into Aunt Polly's driveway and put the truck in park, not turning the engine off. Opening the door, I stopped and turned back to him.

"Thanks, Levi. I needed that," I told him. I jumped out of the truck and shut the door, walking up the front porch stairs. I heard him back out and drive away as I opened the screen door.

"Evan?" Lucy called out after the screen door slammed shut.

"Yep, I'm home," I said, walking into the living room. Lucy was cuddled up on the couch, a book in her lap.

"So? How was your night?"

"It was good," I chuckled. I could tell she was hoping for more, but she wasn't going to get it.

"Just good? Anything else?" she coaxed.

"Uh, Rex was there, and he is completely crazy."

Lucy laughed and agreed as she stood up, stretching.

"Things were smooth here tonight," she told me. "I'm going to head out, but I'll see you tomorrow."

"Thanks, Lucy," I said as I stood up to walk her out. Although Lucy wasn't a guest and could show herself out, I still walked her to the door.

"Thanks, Lucy," I told her as she walked onto the front porch. I followed behind her, careful not to let the screen slam shut.

"You are welcome, Evan. I think you hanging out with Levi is a good thing. He's a wonderful man."

Levi was a wonderful man. He was also a man I loved to fantasize about, and if I let myself get involved with him, it would not end well.

None of my relationships ended well.

I ruined every single one I had ever been in, usually by starting a new one without ending the old one.

I didn't want to do that to Levi. I couldn't.

*

I woke up to the screeching noise of my alarm clock. Reaching over, I shut it off and laid back down, staring at the ceiling. The bed was so comfortable and warm that I didn't want to get up. My thoughts went immediately to Levi. Maybe I could have a relationship with him and not ruin it. But, was he interested in me? I wasn't full of myself, but I was a woman and women know when a man looks at them a certain way. And, I had seen Levi look at me that certain way. His lust-filled eyes and the way he drank in my body told me all I needed to know. He was interested.

I got out of bed and took a shower, putting on a pair of old jeans and a light sweater. It was early summer, but the air had a chill in it and smelled of rain. I loved the rain here. I would be grabbing a book and sitting on the porch swing later.

After leaving the bathroom, I glanced down the hall and noticed Aunt Polly's bedroom door was open. Was it open when I went into the bathroom? Had she gotten out of bed before me?

"Aunt Polly?" I called as I walked into her room. Her bed was unmade with the blankets still messy. I checked her attached bathroom, but no Polly. Her bathrobe hung on the back of the door, so I assumed she did indeed wake up before me and get herself ready for the day.

I walked down the stairs and immediately my sense of smell was attacked with a sickening scent. I knew that smell.

It was blood.

"Aunt Polly!" I called as I raced down the hall into the kitchen where I stopped in my tracks.

A large pool of blood was seeping from behind the kitchen island. I didn't want to walk around and see what I knew in my heart was there, but my feet carried me of their own will.

Lying in that pool of blood was my aunt. Her face was gray, her eyes closed, and I knew I was too late.

I kneeled down next to her and placed my ear over her mouth to check for breathing, but I heard nothing. Gently taking her wrist, I felt for a pulse, even though her skin was cold to the touch. She was in her nightgown, which was drenched in blood, and her long hair was soaking in the pool beneath her. The deep gash in her forehead exposed her skull, and I knew what had happened.

What had I done?

Why didn't I hear her leave her room?

The tears began rolling down my cheeks as the anger and guilt washed over me.

I looked up and saw the chunk of bloody flesh on the corner of the island where she fell. How had I not heard the commotion this would have caused?

I stood up and reached for the phone on the wall, my hands shaking as I dialed for help.

"911, where's your emergency?" the man's voice on the other end asked.

" I need an ambulance at 2201 Cherry Hill Road. My aunt fell, there is so much blood, and she has no pulse," I replied, not recognizing my own voice. I was too calm.

"Okay, miss, I have an ambulance and patrol car on the way. Can you tell me what happened?"

"I... I'm not sure," I said as the tears began to flow again. "I woke up and came downstairs, and I could smell blood in the air. I think she woke up in the middle of the night and fell. She hit her head. She must have been confused; she has dementia," I stammered out, my breathing becoming labored.

"Try to stay as calm as you can. Do you see any sign of a break in or a struggle?" the man asked.

"No, nothing. She was asleep when I went to bed, and I didn't hear her get up," I cried into the phone, the calm being overtaken by fear.

"Okay, stay on the phone with me. The patrol car is one minute out."

That minute felt like hours, but I heard the tires crunching on the gravel and the sound of heavy boots clomping up the steps.

"The officer is here," I told the man.

"Kendrick Sheriff's office!" a loud voice boomed from behind the door.

"Go ahead and answer the door," the voice on the other end of the phone instructed.

I opened the front door and was greeted by a tall man in a tan sheriff's uniform.

"Ma'am," he said as he removed his hat. "I got a call about an accident at this residence."

"Yes, my aunt," I motioned towards the kitchen.

"Polly?" the sheriff asked. I nodded my head.

"Ah hell," he said, pushing by me and quickly walking to the kitchen with me following closely behind him. I still had the phone in my hand and could faintly hear the voice on the other end. Putting it to my ear, I told the dispatcher the sheriff had arrived, and I hung up. Just as I did, I heard the front screen open and shut and more boots coming down the hall. The ambulance had arrived.

"Sheriff Cash, what happened?" a large man in an EMT uniform asked.

"She fell, and I'm not sure how long ago. She's cold, no pulse," Sheriff Cash responded.

I watched in a haze as the EMTs put my aunt's lifeless body on a stretcher and covered her with a sheet. I felt numb as I answered the questions the sheriff asked me. I barely registered when Levi and Rex burst through the door, Levi engulfing me in a hug while Rex spoke with the sheriff.

I was lost.

The rest of the day passed in a blur. Police in and out of the house, asking me questions and taking pictures. Lucy had shown up at some point, staying beside me the entire time, holding my hand and crying. Levi and Rex stayed as well, talking with the sheriff. Every now and then one of them would check on Lucy and me, squeezing our shoulders and telling us everything would be okay.

How? How would everything be okay?

That evening Lucy and I sat on the porch swing in silence, listening to the rain. The house was empty now; everyone was gone.

"How did I not hear her?" I wondered out loud.

The swing stilled.

"Evan, look at me," Lucy demanded, her voice stern.

I turned my head, and my eyes met her puffy ones. I was positive mine were equally as puffy. The tears hadn't stopped.

"Don't you dare blame yourself. This would have happened even if I was here. Do you understand?"

All I could do was nod and stare back out to the road.

My beautiful aunt was gone, and I wasn't ready to say goodbye.

CHAPTER TEN

EVAN

The following weeks were hard. The house felt so empty, even though Lucy, Rex, and Levi were always with me.

The sheriff's office had determined the cause of death to be blood loss from severe head trauma. Sometime during the night, Aunt Polly had come downstairs and most likely tripped on her nightgown, causing her to fall and hit her head on the edge of the island. She was knocked unconscious and bled to death on her kitchen floor.

There was a giant, rust-colored stain on the floor where she had been, and no amount of cleaning could get it out. Levi said he had some flooring at his place and would put it in for me as soon as possible. I was grateful. Looking at that every day was a constant reminder of everything I didn't do for her.

I made funeral arrangements, keeping it small and having her cremated the way she wanted it. Aunt Polly always said she did not want her body buried in the ground for insects to eat. She wanted her ashes kept with her home, so when I was given the urn, I placed her on the mantel of her fireplace. I wanted to do something more with them, but I couldn't think of anything. Eventually, I would though, when my heart didn't hurt as bad.

Lucy went with me to the reading of the will, and to my surprise, Aunt Polly left everything to me.

"Polly Nelson made it very clear that everything is to be left to Evan Susanna Masters in the event of her passing," her lawyer, Mr. Hanson, said as he began to read over the will.

He was an older gentleman with a kind smile and eyes that twinkled. He reminded me of what Santa Claus would look like if he were a younger man.

"Miss Masters, did your aunt ever talk to you about any of this?"

"No, I had no idea," I told him. " I never really wanted to think of her dying."

"Polly was worth almost four million dollars, and her property including the home is sitting right at six hundred thousand. It is all yours, with one stipulation," he said, looking up from the paper in his hands.

Had I really just heard him right? Four million dollars? Where in the hell did she get that kind of money?

"What stipulation is that?" I heard Lucy ask.

"Miss Masters must live in the home as her permanent residence, and the property is to stay in her name."

I smiled a weak smile.

"I wouldn't have it any other way, money or no money," I said.

"And that is why she wanted you to have it," the lawyer said as he nodded approval.

*

"Lucy, did you know she had that much money?", I asked as we drove home.

"Yes, I did," she answered, not taking her eyes off the road.

"How?" I never knew she was rich, but I also knew she didn't work. She would sell flowers from her garden at the farmers market in the summer and sometimes the jams she canned, but there was no way she made millions from that.

"She once told me her grandfather was some sort of oil tycoon, and he sold the business for billions. I guess she inherited some of the money when her father passed away."

How had I never known that? My aunt was my hero in so many ways. I thought we knew everything about each other.

My mother and Polly had different fathers, Aunt Polly being sixteen years older than my mom. My grandmother was the 'other woman' to a man who was also Polly's teacher. From what I knew it was quite the scandal. My mother was the result of the affair, and my grandma became a single mom to two daughters. Aunt Polly left home right after she turned eighteen, but she made sure she had a relationship with her half-sister.

I was conceived from a situation very similar to the one my mother was conceived from, except the man who impregnated my mother was her twelfth-grade history teacher. It was almost as if all the women in my family were destined to create a scandal everywhere they went.

*

It was surreal to check my bank account while paying bills and see my balance in the seven-digit category. I had always struggled financially; teachers did not make very much money.

But if I had a choice between the money and my aunt, I would have taken my aunt.

I had a cashier's check made up, and I presented it to Lucy. She had been there for Polly when I wasn't, and she deserved a bonus. Her eyes bugged when she looked at the amount I wanted to give her.

"This is too much," she protested, trying to hand it back to me.

I gently pushed the check back into her hands.

"No, it's not. Honestly, I don't think it's enough," I told her smiling as I watched the tears roll down her cheeks. I felt my eyes mist up.

"No tears," I said. "This is what Aunt Polly would have thought to be the right thing. She loved you so much."

Lucy nodded her head and began to sob. I grabbed hold of her, hugging her tightly.

"It's a gift. Go on a vacation or something," I suggested as I pulled away from her.

"I think I will," Lucy said as she wiped at her eyes, drying the tears with her shirt sleeve. "My sister lives in Orlando. Maybe I'll go."

"I think that's a great idea," I agreed.

Lucy and I spent the afternoon talking and sharing stories about Aunt Polly. It felt so good to think of the happy times instead of focusing on the fact that she wasn't here anymore. Talking about how amazing she was would keep her in our hearts and thoughts, and both of us never wanted her memory to be forgotten.

I walked Lucy to her car, making her promise to keep in touch.

"Don't you dare let those gardens go to waste," she scolded, nodding her head in the direction of my aunt's prized gardens.

"Oh, I won't. I promise."

"Good thing, Polly would come back from the grave just to smack you," Lucy teased as she got into her car. She started it up, and I swore I could see the tears rolling down her face as she drove away.

*

The strawberries in the little garden Aunt Polly and Levi had put in were ready to be picked. I openly cried as I picked them, heartbroken my aunt wasn't here to see the beautiful berries. They were large and a bright crimson color. When I took a bite out of the first one I picked, I closed my eyes. They were perfect.

I heard the familiar crunch of boots walking up the drive, and I continued to kneel down, picking strawberries.

"So, how did they turn out?" Levi's deep voice asked.

"They're perfect," I replied without turning to look at him. He stood behind me casting a long shadow over the ground. Out the corner of my eye, I saw him stand next to me, inspecting the garden. Kneeling next to me, he began to pick the ripe berries and place them into the bucket I had sitting next to me. I stopped what I was doing to watch him. I watched as he carefully picked one and took a bite out of it, slowly chewing.

"These are amazing," Levi said. He turned to look at me, and I couldn't help but stare at him. I didn't blink as he reached out and wiped away one stray tear. I leaned into his touch, and he pulled me into an embrace. His strong arms encased me in warmth, and I wanted to melt into him.

"Everything will be okay, Evan. I promise."

"I miss her so much it hurts. I feel like I failed her," I cried.

"You didn't fail her. It was an accident that could have happened no matter who was here with her," he said, still holding me tight.

We stayed there like that, kneeling on the ground in front of my aunt's garden, wrapped in each other's arms while I sobbed into his chest. I'd broken down in front of this man I barely knew, and yet, I felt completely safe and comfortable.

I felt like in his arms was where I belonged.

We spent the rest of the day on the porch swing, eating the strawberries we'd picked. We didn't talk much, just sat side by side and watched the fields across from the home that was now mine. I had never felt so at ease with a man in my life. There was something about Levi. I'd heard of people feeling like they had always known someone they just met, but I had never experienced it, until now.

The sun was beginning to set, and we hadn't moved from the porch swing. Levi seemed to sense that I just wanted to share my quiet with someone. He never said anything unless I did, and he never pried or told me shit I didn't want to hear. He was just there, sitting beside me.

It was exactly what I had needed.

We watched as Rex pulled into his driveway, one headlight out on his beat up old Nova.

"I'm going to get home before he raids all of my beer and food," Levi said as he stood up. "You okay?"

I nodded, saying nothing. I felt as Levi put his index finger under my chin and lifted my head, so my gaze met his. It was an intimate gesture, one I had only read about in books. I had never had a man treat me as gently as Levi did.

"I'm right across the road if you need anything, and I mean anything. Got it?" his voice had a sternness to it that made my stomach clench and the heat between my legs become more aware of his presence.

"Yes, I got it," I replied.

Levi smiled at me and turned to leave.

"Thanks, Levi," I called after him.

Once again, as if he knew me, he didn't make an issue out of my words. Instead, he kept walking as he put his hand in the air and gave me a thumbs up.

I needed to be more careful around that man. I needed to keep my guard up, or I might just let him in.

Or, was he in already?

65

CHAPTER ELEVEN

LEVI

I had to play it cool with Evan. She wasn't like other women. She wasn't looking for a husband or a sugar daddy. She wasn't looking for anything. She was just Evan. Her strength was one of my biggest turn-ons, but ever since Polly died, Evan had closed in on herself.

She blamed herself for the accident, but everyone around her knew she wasn't to blame. It would have happened regardless of who was there that night.

The medical examiner estimated the fall happened in the very early hours of the morning, around two or three. A time of day most people are still asleep, including Polly. I knew her schedule, and old girl slept in every single morning. There had been more than one occasion where I had gone over in the morning to check in on her and Lucy before heading out to a job for the day and Polly was still asleep.

I missed her. Polly had become family to me over the years, and I loved her. It hurt to go over and not see her in her garden or sitting on her porch. So, the day I looked out and saw Evan kneeling down in front of the strawberry garden I felt drawn to her. She needed someone to be with her, and that someone needed to be me.

She was mine. She just didn't know it yet.

But, I did. She was meant to be mine.

That night I spent my time trying to keep Evan from my thoughts. I washed my work truck and got the trailer loaded up for a big dig out Rex and I were scheduled to do. I washed out the coolers before loading them up, but I found myself constantly looking across the road to the old farmhouse that was lit up like a Christmas tree. I saw movement in one of the upstairs windows and a shadow pass by, and at that moment, I knew Evan was watching me, too.

"Oh yeah, you are mine," I said to no one as I continued to load the truck.

*

"So, have you fucked her yet?" Rex asked as we drove home after a long day of digging. I was dirty and tired and not in the mood to answer any of his questions.

"It's none of your fucking business, but no, I haven't. Evan isn't like that."

"Oh, yeah she is," Rex snorted. "I can see it written all over that face of hers. She is like that."

It pissed me the fuck off that Rex assumed he knew Evan. It pissed me the fuck off when he mentioned her. He had no right to her and talking about her to me rubbed me the wrong way. I had known Rex forever, and I loved him, but I felt nothing but possessive when it came to Evan.

"And exactly what is written all over her face?" I questioned as we turned down the road leading to my house.

"You can't see it, man? She has that sex-crazed look that truly sex crazed chicks try to hide."

"Jesus, you are so fucked up," I replied.

"Nah, it's true. The ones who throw it out there are boring as shit in bed. The ones who hide it are the ones to watch out for. Those are the ones who will let you come on their face and ask for more."

I shook my head, laughing. One thing Rex was always good for was a laugh.

"What? It's nothing to laugh about, dude. Evan is slutty. She just keeps that slut chained up in the basement. You are just the man to unlock those chains," Rex said as we pulled into my driveway.

I killed the lights and got out of the truck.

"You coming in?" I asked Rex as I walked up the front steps.

"Nope, I'm heading home," he told me. Rex walked over to his car, throwing his stuff in through the open window. He opened the driver side door, got in, and fired up his beat up old Nova. The thing was ugly, but Rex had built the shit out of the motor, and it sounded like a beast. Hanging his head out his window, he smiled at me.

"Why don't you go get cleaned up and go to your neighbor's and break her out of those chains?" And with that, he threw it in reverse, turned around, and gunned it out of the drive, spraying gravel as he went.

Fucker, now I would have to smooth out the driveway, again.

The next morning, I woke up on my couch, the TV still on and the half-eaten pizza I had ordered the night before on the coffee table. After I had showered and put on a pair of sweats, I was in no mood to make anything to eat. And after everything Rex had put in my head about Evan, I was in no shape to go over to her house.

Rex was a lot of things, and one of those things was observant. He came across as an arrogant asshole who was so full of himself that he was hard to be around sometimes, but he was smart. And, he watched everything and everyone. He was usually spot on about people.

Something told me he was right about Evan. I wouldn't use the term slut about her, but there was something about her that said she was a very sexual girl. I was okay with that, but for the first time ever I didn't want it to be all about sex. I liked Evan. I wanted to know her. I wanted to fuck her, there was no way around that. But after I fucked her, I wanted to sleep next to her and wake up and make her breakfast.

Shit, I had never wanted that with another woman.

Thinking about her had my dick so fucking hard it ached. It seemed to be that way every single fucking morning I woke up knowing she was just across the road from me. I pictured her sleeping in a little tank top and panties, her full tits on display and her long legs bare. I wanted to be in between those legs.

My shower ended up being a jerk fest that morning. I felt better when I got out, but the ache in my balls was still there.

I needed to see her.

I put on my sweats and headed back downstairs. It was early on a Saturday morning, and the day was promising to be a hot and humid one. I shut the heavy curtains to keep the cool air that was blowing in. When I had bought the house, I did a full renovation on it, including having central air installed. It wasn't cheap, but it was worth it, especially after a long ass day running equipment in the heat.

Polly's house had no air in it. I used to bring her over to my place on days it was really hot, especially on the weekends. Lucy was off those days, and I didn't like the weekend nurses. Well, I may have liked one or two of them once or twice after Polly went to bed. But that's what was so shady about them. They were okay with fucking a stranger while their patient slept down the hall.

I ended up heading to the gym for a couple hours, and when I got home, I didn't see Evan's car in her driveway. It was fucking hot as balls outside, so I changed into a pair of shorts, threw on my running shoes, and ran out towards the swimming hole in Polly's creek. She always called it her 'criver,' and I loved that place in the summer.

As I approached, I saw someone was already there. A blanket was laid out, and a long, curvy body in a black string bikini that barely covered a fucking thing was laying on it. Her hair was piled on top of her head, and she was on her stomach, her legs stretched out behind her as she read a beat up looking paperback book.

Fuck me.

"Hey," I called out, not wanting to startle her. She was jumpy and didn't like being snuck up on. I watched as she turned her body, one of her gorgeous round tits half hanging out of the small triangle that hardly covered what I imagined to be a perfect nipple. She smiled.

"Hey yourself," Evan said as she turned and sat up, straightening out her top. "What are you doing out here?"

"It's fucking hot, and I came here to get wet."

I saw the tiny glimmer in her eye, the one that said she was already wet.

Fucking Rex. I hated it when he was right.

Kicking off my shoes, I ran towards the water, launching myself off the high bank, doing a front flip and splashing into the cool water. I surfaced and found Evan standing on the bank.

"I never took you for a show-off." She laughed and then jumped in. Swimming over to where I could touch, I waited for her to surface. When she did, she swam over to where I was and stood next to me.

"I love it here," she told me.

"Me, too."

Evan waded down a bit further to a spot where she could sit along the sandy bank and keep her legs in the water. The water moved faster there, and it washed over her. I came and sat next to her. Once again, we sat in silence.

Evan slowly reached up and pulled her hair back into one of her sloppy buns, the ones I thought looked sexy as hell on her. She sat back and looked up, watching the clouds. I couldn't help but watch her.

"What are you looking at?" she asked, never taking her eyes off the clouds.

"You," I blurted out before I even knew what I wanted to say.

She turned her head, and I was met with the most beautiful, haunted, hazel eyes I had ever seen.

"Why?" she whispered.

"Because I want to fucking kiss you," I confessed, my eyes never leaving hers.

Neither of us spoke. Neither of us looked away.

I snaked my hand around the back of her neck and pulled her closer to me, her breath on my lips. I held her there, less than an inch from me waiting for her to say no.

She didn't.

I pulled her to me once more, and our lips met.

She was soft, so soft I had to hold back. I didn't want to be soft with her, but I didn't want to scare her away. Not the first time I touched her.

I parted her lips with my tongue, making my way into her mouth. I found her tongue and began a slow, sensual dance. Evan's chest began to rise and fall harder, and I felt the moment she caved, crushing her body to mine and tangling her hands in my hair.

The kiss became more than a kiss. We were literally fucking each other's mouths with our tongues.

I reached around Evan and pulled her onto my lap, turning her so she straddled me and I could press my hard cock against her, relieving some of the pressure that never seemed to leave. She moaned into my mouth.

"Levi," she panted, "I can't. Not yet."

Her body betrayed her as she began to grind on me. It was fucking hot as hell.

Evan threw her head back as we continued to dry fuck through the little bit of fabric that separated us. I grabbed her head, bringing her lips back to mine as I moved against her. I knew the head of my cock was rubbing against her clit, and she was close to orgasming. So was I.

"Keep going, baby," I said as I kissed along her neck. She was so fucking beautiful.

Evan continued to ride me, and I felt my balls tighten up.

"You're making me come," I said into her mouth as she bit my lip.

"Come," she whimpered. "Because so am I."

I felt it as I shot hot semen all over myself, in my shorts, like a teenaged fucking boy. I could feel the heat coming from Evan's pussy through them as well and holy shit.

I kissed her lips again, knowing it wouldn't be the last one for the day. When she tried to pull away from me, I held her tighter. She looked at me, and I smirked, bringing a smile to her lips. I kissed her one more time.

"That," I sighed, "was the hottest fucking thing I have ever done."

CHAPTER TWELVE

EVAN

I sat, straddling Levi after we dry fucked on the bank of my creek. What the hell was I thinking?

The truth is I wasn't thinking, and that was a problem.

I'd tried to wiggle out of his hold, but Levi held me to him. I liked the way I felt in his arms. Safe. Protected. He was so big, his frame menacing and strong, but at the same time, he was caring and soft. No man had ever brought any type of feeling out of me. It was always physical. No emotions. But Levi? I felt something, something real. Something I couldn't ignore.

I wanted to be with him.

And not just for sex. I wanted to know him.

And it scared the hell out of me.

"That was the hottest fucking thing I have ever done," Levi quietly murmured after kissing me again.

"Same," I sighed into his mouth. I didn't want to let go of him.

Levi pulled back and looked at me, his eyes filled with more lust than I had ever seen. Damn, he was sexy. His chest was broad, and his arms were so thick that I didn't think I could get both hands around one. His stomach wasn't ripped, but there was a faint six-pack, and I wanted to lick every inch of him.

"Hey," Levi said, getting my attention back to his eyes.

"Hmmm?" I was suddenly sleepy, and my body felt like rubber. The side effects of a good orgasm.

"Where are you right now?"

"I am right here, right now," I replied, still holding on to him.

"I want to spend the day with you. No expectations. I know you aren't ready for more, and I'm okay with that, for now," he said.

He didn't expect me to fuck him. He just wanted to spend time with me.

"What's wrong with you?" I thought out loud. I hadn't meant to ask it.

Levi laughed. "What do you mean?"

"No guy is ever okay with not fucking," I pointed out.

He leaned in, kissing me again as he lifted me from his lap. He stood up and pulled me with him, grabbing me and wrapping his arms around me.

"I'm not every guy. I don't want to deal with the pointless bullshit. I fucking like you, Evan. I have ever since that first time I met you. You're strong and not some helpless twat I can't stand being around. So, yes, I want to spend time with you, the first woman who has actually held my attention," he confessed.

I smiled, my eyes locked on his.

"Okay."

The rest of the day we spent at the criver, swimming, laughing and kissing. So much kissing.

It was bliss.

But, my traitorous brain kept telling me it was all too good to be true. That a woman like me didn't deserve happiness. All the bad decisions I had made, all the low life men I had allowed in my bed. I was a terrible person wearing the skin of someone who could be good.

I didn't deserve this man. I didn't deserve any man, not after my past. Memories of avoiding Louis after the day at the tree clouded my mind.

I didn't know what to tell Aunt Polly, so I never said a word. She probably wouldn't believe me anyway. Why would she? He was the sheriff, the guy the whole town thought was a hero or something.

He would sit across from me at the table for dinner, and I could feel his eyes on me, watching me. I never looked up from my plate, and as soon as I was done, I would excuse myself from the table and start washing the dishes. As soon as I was done with that, I would either cling to my aunt's side or hide in my room for the night.

The hardest time was when Aunt Polly went to play Bunco with her friends. I had to try and busy myself somehow. I usually went across the road and hung out with Della Richardson, my only friend in Kendrick.

"Do you want to spend the night?", Della asked as we laid on her bed looking through her Tiger Beat magazines and drooling over Leo and n'Sync.

"Really?"

"Yeah! We can stay up late and watch movies downstairs after my parents go to bed," she exclaimed.

"I do, but I have to ask my aunt, and she is playing Bunco tonight," I told her, still thumbing through the magazine.

"So, she is at Mrs. Matthews' house? My mom has her number. Call and ask."

We ran downstairs to the kitchen, finding Della's mom's phone list and dialing Mrs. Matthews' house. I asked for my aunt, assuring Mrs. Matthews everything was okay before she put Aunt Polly on.

"Evan? Is everything okay?" Aunt Polly asked, a hint of worry in her voice.

"Yes, I wanted to ask if I could sleep over at Della's tonight."

"Yeah, that would be fine, sweetheart. Are her parents' home?"

"Yep, do you want to talk to her mom?" I offered.

"I do; I just want to be sure she is okay with you staying," Aunt Polly told me.

Della called for her mom, and I handed her the phone when she came into the kitchen. We stood there as she talked to my aunt. Once she hung up and said it was fine that I was there, Della and I ran across the road to my house to get my clothes for the night.

The lights were on and the door open; the house looked like the picture of inviting.

We burst through the front door, laughing and came to a stop. Louis had come into the front hall from the kitchen, most likely from the commotion Della and I had caused when we came in. His face gave away nothing, and I couldn't tell if he was mad.

"What are you two girls up to?" he slurred, his eyes wandering up and down Della, who was in a pair of spandex shorts and a tank top. I stood in front of her, blocking his view.

"We came over to get my clothes for a sleepover," I replied.

"Who told you that was okay?"

"We called Aunt Polly, and Della's mom talked to her," I said, straightening my spine. As if the mention of another adult brought him out of whatever power trip he was on, he walked into the living room and sat down. I noticed the empty beer cans littering the coffee table; he had been drinking for a while.

"Okay, then." His eyes went to the TV, and he picked up an unopened beer, popped the top, and took three long pulls from it. I grabbed Della by the arm and ran upstairs, shutting my door behind us.

"What's his problem?" Della asked as she plopped down on my bed.

"I don't know. He creeps me out. I don't get why my aunt married him," I said as I grabbed clothes out of my dresser and shoved them into a backpack.

"Me, either. He watches me and my mom, and it's so gross."

"Yeah, he is gross," I confirmed. I couldn't tell Della everything; I was too embarrassed. But, knowing my friend didn't like him made me feel like I had someone on my side.

"How can you stand being in the same house as him?" Della asked.

"I can't. That's why we are going to yours."

78

CHAPTER THIRTEEN

EVAN

"You have been spending a lot of time with Levi," Lucy grinned as we sat out back. The day was hot as hell, and the humidity made our clothes stick to us. We were both wearing light sundresses as we sat in the shade. I had my hair piled on top of my head, and I could feel the sweat from my scalp trickle down my neck.

I had been spending a lot of time with Levi, and he had been true to his word. He hadn't attempted to have sex with me, although we had some very hot make-out sessions. He was so fucking sexy, and the fact he was the one putting the brakes on sex made him even hotter.

It was just what I needed. Someone who cared enough not to make me feel cheap and used.

Someone I could see myself with.

Someone I was scared of.

Someone that made me feel.

"Yeah," was all I said, avoiding eye contact.

Lucy had stayed a constant ever since Aunt Polly died, and I was grateful for her. She had helped me with the legal shit and with the funeral. I wouldn't have even known where to start without her. And now, she was here, ever observant and asking about Levi.

"So," she coaxed, "are you two an item?"

I hope so, I thought.

"We're just friends, Lucy," I laughed.

"Just friends, hm?" Lucy teased, arching an eyebrow.

"Yes, friends," I reasserted, even though it was a complete lie. Friends don't make each other come with their hands.

"Well, maybe we should have your friend over for dinner. It was something Polly did weekly. She would have Levi and Rex over."

Lucy was testing me, and I knew it. So, I called her bluff.

"That's cool, but it's so damn hot out what are we going to cook?"

"I'm a barbeque master, so don't worry about that. Make a salad and cut up a watermelon, and we're in business." She smiled.

Lucy called Levi and invited him and Rex, and of course, he said they would love to come. I immediately texted him and told him Lucy didn't know we had been seeing each other and I wasn't ready for her to know.

He responded with a short "K."

I made a broccoli salad and cut up a watermelon while Lucy sat out back, barbequing chicken and humming to herself. There was no denying it was a perfect day. The only thing missing was Aunt Polly, but as cliché as it sounded, I felt her all around me. Just being in her home made me feel at ease, knowing how much she loved the place. I was the right person to leave it to; she knew I would never sell it. I could never sell it.

Levi and Rex came over, and dinner was delicious. Lucy really was a barbeque master. The four of us sat out back, full of the good food and sipping on the mojitos Rex had made.

The conversation was flowing, talking about Polly and the stories that made us laugh. Rex told us some of his stories, and Lucy and I sat there a little dumbfounded.

"And so, this chick, I don't fucking remember her name, anyhow, this chick climbed under the table and started blowing me while I was sitting across from her boyfriend. He was so wasted he didn't even realize she was gone from the table," Rex barked, laughing loudly at his own story.

"Man, you're a fucking pig," Levi snorted, taking a drink of his beer.

Levi hadn't looked at me much all evening, and I wondered what was wrong. I loved his eyes on me, and I needed them on me tonight.

I stood up, clearing the table and heading inside. I walked into the kitchen and placed the dirty dishes in the sink, filling it with hot, soapy water. I spun when I heard the back screen slam shut, expecting Levi. But instead, I found Rex, his hands loaded with more dishes.

"Oh, thanks, Rex." I smiled, turning to the sink to begin washing. I felt Rex approach and stand to my side. I turned and found his eyes burning through me.

"What's going on, Evan?" Rex demanded.

"What do you mean?"

He shook his head and sighed. "You see that guy out there?" He motioned to the back door where I could see Levi and Lucy still sitting at the table talking.

"Yes," I said, wondering what he was getting at.

"Well, that guy is all the fucking family I have, and he is starting to fall hard for a chick who has so many walls up he can't get through even one of them. So, that chick needs to either shit or get off the pot, if you know what I mean."

Rex never beat around the bush, he always said whatever he was thinking. A quality I admired about him, except right now.

"I know what you mean," I whispered, and my eyes averted to the ground.

"If you're that fucked up, Evan, then you need to be done with whatever it is you are doing and let him do his thing. He's had enough bad shit happen in his life. He doesn't need something that could be good turn into shit. Figure it out."

And with that, Rex walked out of the kitchen and back to Levi and Lucy, laughing as if nothing was wrong.

As much as I hated to admit it, Rex was right. I needed to figure it out.

I didn't know why I had so many walls up for Levi. He had proven over and over he was a good man. A man I trusted. The *first* man I had ever trusted. So, why was I pushing him away?

I wanted to be with him, and he made no secret about wanting to be with me. Why was I hiding how I felt?

Because I was fucked up. I was so scared of feeling that I was completely ruining something I knew was right. I felt it the first time I met him.

Levi was right for me.

It was why I was so scared. Could I have someone who brought me happiness and peace? Why would I ever deserve that?

Because I did.

I deserved love.

After everyone left, I went upstairs and showered, towel drying my thick hair so it would dry in long waves. I left my face makeup free as I sprayed a light scent on my neck and wrists. I found my pink lacy bra and panty set and put them on as I prepared myself to knock down a few walls.

I picked up my cell and sent a text to Levi.

Me: come back plz

Levi: everything ok

Me: fine. I just want to see you

Levi: omw

Me: door's open

After looking in the mirror once more, I waited. When I heard the front door close, I let out a breath I hadn't realized I was holding.

"Evan?" I heard Levi call out.

I walked down the steps, counting each one as I stepped to the next. My breathing was deep, trying to keep myself calm as Levi came into view. His eyes widened when he saw me, and a little smile played on his lips. He drank in every inch of my body until his eyes came back to meet mine.

He said nothing as I walked to him, standing inches from him.

"Holy shit," he approved.

I brought my arms up and around his neck, pulling him a little closer.

"I want you to stay with me tonight," I whispered.

"Are you sure?"

Just the fact that he cared enough to make sure this was what I wanted made me want him even more.

"I had a revelation tonight, and I am done pushing you away. I want you, Levi. I want everyone to know how much I want you. No more hiding, no more waiting," I confessed.

I barely had the last word out before he crushed his lips to mine. His hands sliding down my back to my ass, cupping each cheek and squeezing. He lifted me slightly, and I wrapped my legs around him as he began to effortlessly walk up the steps.

"Which room is yours?" he breathed into my mouth.

"Last door on the left," I sighed, biting his bottom lip.

Levi walked down the hall, kicking the door open and slamming it shut behind him as he walked in. He eased me down until I was standing in front of him.

"Evan, I want you so fucking bad, but I need to know this is what you want. Rex told me what he said to you," Levi admitted.

I smiled.

"And, what Rex said to me was exactly what I needed. You should thank him, tomorrow," I smirked. Grabbing the hem of Levi's shirt, I lifted it, prompting him to raise his arms so I could pull it off. I loved his body—big, fierce and tattooed. His chest was broad, and across it was a black and white tattoo of a pitchfork and tail with the words 'hell is empty and all the devils are here' scrawled across it. I ran my fingers over it, causing his skin to break out in goose bumps.

Levi took my face in his hands and kissed me. This kiss was different than the others we had shared. This kiss was soft, possessive.

This kiss claimed me.

I reached down and unzipped his jeans as he walked me backwards to the bed. I sat when I felt the backs of my knees hit, and he stood before me. I watched as he kicked off his already unlaced boots. He slid his jeans down his thick, toned legs, and I marveled in the bulge I was greeted with through his boxer briefs. I had felt him through our clothes numerous times, but seeing it, knowing it was going to be in me tonight had me vibrating with anticipation.

Levi crawled on top of me, pressing his body into mine, and I loved the heaviness of him on me. I loved how strong he was and how he could ruin me if he wanted, but knowing he wouldn't.

He kissed me again, harder this time, and my body hummed. I kissed him back, burying my fingers in his wavy, thick hair and wrapping my legs around his waist. His hand skimmed up the back of my thigh, coming to rest on my ass. He pressed himself into me, and I brought my hips up, moaning into his mouth.

"Levi," I panted, breaking the connection as I ran my hands down and squeezed his ass.

"Yeah, baby?" he groaned.

"I want you so fucking bad," I confessed, taking his bottom lip and sucking on it. He pulled back and smirked, slowly inching down my body, grabbing the waistband of my pink panties and dragging them all the way down my legs. He kneeled down in between my ankles, taking them in his large hands and kissing the tips of my toes.

In one swift move, he spread my legs apart, baring me to him. I felt nothing but excitement as he kissed and nipped at my inner thigh as he worked his way up.

My breathing became labored, the anticipation growing more than I could bear.

"Levi," I moaned, barely recognizing my own voice.

"Yes, baby? What do you want? Tell me," he coaxed, still running his hands up and down my inner thighs, barely touching my pussy and then backing off. It was torture.

"You," I cried. "I want you!"

"Tell me," he growled, his hand splayed across my lower stomach, holding me in place.

"My pussy, Levi, lick my pussy."

"Was that so hard?" he asked, his voice deep and throaty. I looked down my body and watched as he lowered his head, and I could feel his hot breath on me, blowing on my core.

With one fluid motion, he licked me, his tongue probing my folds.

Holy fucking shit.

He continued to hold me down as he licked me over and over again, bringing me to the edge and backing off only to do it all over again. As if that wasn't enough, he added a finger, pushing one thick digit into me and hooking it, finding that spot. That one spot that can make a woman come undone, which was exactly what I did.

"Oh fuck, Levi!" I cried as I felt the tightening in my lower body, the tell-tale sign I was going to come.

Then, he sucked my clit, and that was the end. I felt the warmth between my legs gush, and my body shuddered as I orgasmed harder than I ever had.

"Yes, baby. Fuck yes," Levi panted as he watched me ride out the last wave of my orgasm.

He climbed up my body, palming my breasts like he knew they needed to be touched. He leaned down and kissed me, and I could taste myself on his lips.

"You're a squirter." He smiled.

"What?" I squeaked, not sure how to react.

"No, Evan, it's fucking hot," Levi reassured me as he grabbed my hand, bringing it to his cock. Pulling his boxer briefs off, he wrapped my hand around his very thick shaft.

"Do you feel how fucking hard I am?" he asked, and I nodded. "It's from watching you. You do this to me."

"I need you in me," I almost whined.

He got up from the bed, his thick cock jutting out in front of him as he leaned down, grabbing his jeans from the floor. He was getting a condom, something I hadn't even thought about, and that one small act from this man made me realize I was going to do anything he wanted tonight.

He walked back to me, stroking his erection as his eyes never left mine. My mouth was literally watering at the sight of him. I sat up and unclasped the back of my bra, freeing my tender breasts. I saw the look of appreciation in Levi's eyes as he took me in.

"You are so fucking gorgeous. Do you know that?" he asked as he crawled onto the bed, laying back and pulling me onto him until I was straddling him. His cock stood up, his warmth resting against my lower stomach. I watched as Levi ripped the packet open, pulling the condom out and rolling it on. He made putting a damn condom on hot.

His eyes stayed on mine as he lifted me up, positioning my opening over the tip of his erection.

Slowly, I lowered myself onto him, and, oh my god, he filled me like no other man.

A long, low moan came from my throat as I felt our bodies meet. I stilled for a second, letting my pussy adjust to him. He was so thick that I swore I could feel every vein on his cock pulse inside of me.

"Move, baby, fuck me," Levi groaned.

Lifting myself up, I lowered again and again until we were rocking back and forth together. Levi had sat up, wrapping one arm around my back, holding me to him as he thrust up as I came down.

The fucking was hard, but I could feel the emotions swarming between us.

This was more than fucking.

This was us, claiming each other.

This was us, loving each other.

Our bodies were slick with sweat, the air still warm from the humid day, but we didn't seem to notice. We held onto each other, desperately thrusting, kissing, biting, and sucking on one another. I never wanted him to leave my body.

I could feel him stiffen and knew he was close. I wanted to see him come undone.

"Come, Levi," I cried as I continued to ride his cock. "Come in me!"

With one final thrust, I felt him throb, my walls clenching around him as he spurted into the condom.

I stilled, resting my forehead against his, and we stayed like that as our breathing calmed. When I pulled back to look at Levi, I was met with steel gray eyes that seemed to be shining. I leaned down and kissed him, his hands fisting into my wild hair as he devoured my mouth.

When our kiss broke, I smiled at him, and he smiled back.

"That was fucking amazing," he said, his hair a mess and his face looking younger, relaxed.

He kissed me one more time.

"I don't ever want to let you go, Evan. You're mine," Levi challenged.

All I could do was stare at him and say the first thing that came to mind.

"Yes, I am."

CHAPTER FOURTEEN

LEVI

The sight of Evan riding me like a fucking champion was the sexiest thing I had seen in a very long time. Maybe even ever. Her cries had been low, and her body responded to every touch. It was almost as if her body knew it belonged with mine.

I disposed of the condom and splashed my face with some cold water in Evan's bathroom. Damn, the house was warm, the effect of no air conditioning. I never understood why Polly didn't have central air installed.

When I returned to the bedroom, I found Evan almost asleep, a thin sheet covering her lush body. I turned out the light and joined her, ignoring the warmth and tucking her into me. I had always despised sleeping next to a woman I had just fucked, but with Evan, I didn't want to let her go.

There was no way this was going to be just a fuck.

I wanted her in my life.

Not one woman had ever held my attention in the past.

One and done, usually.

But this woman, there was something more to her. Something darker than she let on. And, I was drawn to her because of it. Her dark complimented mine, her lies and secrets intertwined with mine, and we would work because of it.

I wanted to know all of her secrets, and I wanted to tell her mine.

*

"I see you freed your neighbor from her chains," Rex called out the next morning as he watched me walk up to my house from my front porch.

I said nothing as I unlocked the front door and headed inside.

Rex followed.

"So?" he asked, an eyebrow raised waiting for me to spill the details.

"So, what?" I growled.

I had spent the night with Evan, waking up and driving into her one more time before I had to leave for work. Before I left, I told her to be ready by three, promising to take her on a date she wouldn't forget.

"So, how was she?" Rex pressed, his eyes wide as he tried to stare me down. He looked semi-crazed.

"I am not going to talk about my sex life, especially with you," I let him know as I walked into the mudroom to retrieve my work boots.

"Why not with me? I am a self-proclaimed love expert."

Now that made me laugh.

"You? A love expert?"

"Hell, yes me. I have experienced all sorts of love. Black love, white love, two at a time love, strapped to a rubber sheet love," he started naming off all his *love* experience.

"Yeah, not the fucking same," I had to stop him before he divulged more details than any one person should ever hear.

"Hey dude, love isn't gay if there's a chick in the middle. So what if I may or may not have jerked him off? It was beautiful," Rex claimed.

"Look, you already know what happened, so I don't need to tell you anything more than I like this girl. I plan on taking her out tonight," I told him as we walked out the back door to my shop. Releasing the bay doors, they opened loudly, exposing my work truck with the trailer already loaded on.

"You taking her to the harvest festival tonight?" Rex asked as he opened the passenger door to the truck.

"Yep."

"Good, come by the dunk tank. I need all the money I can get."

Rex ran a dunk tank every year, raising money for whatever kids sport needed it. This year, it was the girls T-ball team's uniforms. He usually made a small fortune, almost everyone in line was a woman who he'd pissed off. It was a brilliant plan on his part.

*

The day had gone smoothly, doing a dig out for the Johnston's new shop. We only worked for five hours, getting the ground level for the concrete to be poured. The air was

93

humid making the dirt stick to every exposed surface on my skin. I had a shower installed in my mudroom just for this purpose, so when I got home, the first thing I did was strip my clothes off and get in.

I found myself hurrying through it so I could get over to Evan's place.

As I picked up my cell to text her, I knew I was dangerously close to becoming pussy whipped, and I was okay with that.

Me: r u almost ready?

Evan: yep!

Me: I will come get u

Evan: no- I can walk over.

Me: ok.

I watched as she walked up my driveway, her caramel hair loose and shining in the late day sun. She was wearing a long, wine-colored sundress with thin straps and a pair of flip-flops, and she looked gorgeous. She looked like the definition of wild and free.

I walked off the steps and greeted her, taking her into my arms and kissing her like I hadn't seen her in weeks.

"What's this all about?" she asked as I kissed her neck.

"Just claiming my woman."

"You know, I should be backing away from this whole caveman vibe you have going, but I kind of like it," she teased.

"Good," I replied, taking her hand and leading her to my truck. I opened the passenger door for her and helped her up, making sure I placed my hands firmly on her ass as I did.

She laughed as she scooted into the seat, and I shut the door behind her. I loved the sound of her laugh.

"So? Where are we going?" she asked as I started the truck.

"When was the last time you went to the Kendrick Harvest Festival?"

"Seriously? Oh my gosh! I haven't been since I was twelve!"

"That's where we're heading. It's a tradition, and now that you live here, it's time to get your town traditions started.

CHAPER FIFTEEN

EVAN

We pulled into the dirt parking lot, and Levi parked, turning the truck off and getting out to come around and open my door. Helping me out, he took my hand and led me into the festival.

The fairway was lit up with carnival games, and the smell of food hung heavy in the air.

It felt as if nothing had changed since the last time I was there.

We walked through as Levi said hello to just about everyone. I smiled politely as he introduced me to some of the people I didn't know, and he was patient and courteous as I said hello to some of my aunt's old friends. The entire town was there, so my relationship status with Levi would no longer be a secret. Gossip seemed to carry much faster the smaller the town was.

"You hungry?" Levi asked as we approached the food carts.

"Yes, I plan on eating the biggest elephant ear and washing it down with a strawberry milkshake," I told him, making him laugh and pull me to him.

We made our way to the dunk tank, and Levi hadn't been kidding. The line was long, made up of mostly women, a few men, and some kids. Rex sat on the platform above the water taunting the woman who was up next.

"Oh, hey there, Heather," Rex said as the dark-haired woman was handed three softballs.

"Hi, Rex," she sneered. She rocketed the first ball and hit the bullseye, dunking Rex into the water.

He came up sputtering and coughing. Putting the platform back into place, he hopped back onto it and smiled widely.

"I forgot you were a softball pitcher." Rex laughed right before he went back into the water after she threw the next ball.

It made me laugh.

"He doesn't make a lot of friends, does he?" I asked Levi as we watched Rex go in on Heather's third throw.

"Nope."

*

The evening was warm and perfect, and Levi made our date the best I had ever been on. We looked at all the barn animals, looked at an exhibit on bee-keeping, ate more food, watched Rex get dunked a couple more times, checked out a local band playing on the main stage, and held hands the entire time.

"I'm going to use the restroom," I told him when I saw a sign for the ladies' room.

"Okay, I'll be right here."

I walked into the brightly-lit bathroom and found an empty stall. Once I was done, I went to the sink and began washing my hands. I looked up to check my face in the mirror and noticed a gaunt-faced woman standing behind me, watching me in the mirror. Her eyes went wide when our stares locked.

I knew her.

"Della?" I said, turning around.

She said nothing as she continued to stand there, a look of hurt and pain on her once pretty face.

"Della Richardson?"

I watched her face change as recognition set in.

"Evan? I wondered if that was you," Della said, her voice rough and gravely. "What are you doing back in Kendrick?"

"Aunt Polly died and left me her home."

Della narrowed her eyes.

"Why do you want it? You never came back, so I figured you hated it here," she spat the words at me.

If she only knew she was somewhat correct.

"I didn't hate it here. I just didn't want to come anymore."

"Why?" Della demanded.

"I just didn't."

"Why? What happened that made you not want to come back?" Della practically yelled. Her eyes began to glisten before the first tear streaked down her cheek. She lunged forward, grabbing me by my forearms.

"Tell me!"

"Let go, Della!" I ripped my arms from her frail grasp, and I noticed the sores that decorated her skin. It looked like she had been picking at them, and I noticed she had them on her face, as well.

"What happened to you?" I asked her as she backed away. Her tears of sadness turned into anger in an instant.

"Just get the fuck out of here, Evan Masters. You can't even begin to understand what happened to me. Go live your perfect fucking life," Della fumed at me.

I said nothing else as I turned and walked out of the bathroom, finding Levi talking with a man. I walked over to him and watched as Della left the bathroom. Her eyes never left mine as she walked by.

"Hey," I said as I took his hand. He looked at me, and instantly his mood shifted.

"Everything okay?" he asked, sensing something was wrong.

"Yeah, fine," I lied. I turned my attention to the man he was talking to and noticed he was in a sheriff's uniform.

"Evan, you remember Sheriff Cash? I think you can be formally introduced. Brendan, this is Evan Masters," Levi said.

Sheriff Cash put his hand out for me to shake.

"It's nice to actually meet you, Sheriff Cash," I told him as I placed my hand in his, smiling at the man who was so kind the day Aunt Polly died.

"Just call me Brendan," he smiled at me. He was handsome. He appeared to be a little older than Levi, maybe in his early forties. His blond hair was neatly cut, and he was cleanly shaven. His smile was warm and reached his baby blue eyes that had the fine lines of aging wrapped around them. He was distinguished looking.

"Okay," I laughed, "it's nice to meet you, Brendan."

"So, I hear you are Levi's new old lady?"

I looked from Brendan to Levi, and he just shrugged.

"News travels fast around here," I remarked.

"You know it," Brendan agreed. He put his hand out, shaking Levi's before he turned his attention back to me.

"I better get to walking around and doing my job. It was nice to meet you, Evan," he said, nodding at me. He turned and walked into the crowd, greeting people and shaking more hands.

"He seems nice," I said as we started walking.

"What was wrong when you came out of the bathroom?"

It appeared that Levi was observant.

"I ran into Della Richardson. What happened to her?"

"Oh, you know, meth, meth and more meth. That's the reason I bought her parents' home. They needed money for rehab and court fines. That girl is a walking disappointment. But, I got a good deal on their place, and I think they were able to put her through rehab a few times with the money they got."

"I couldn't believe it was really her. She was my friend when we were kids, but the last summer I was here, she wouldn't see me," I told him.

"That's what meth does to people. Steer clear of her, you got me?" Levi demanded.

"Yeah, I got you."

*

The next couple of days after my run-in with Della at the festival were the hottest of the summer. Levi had me staying over at his house where there was air conditioning.

I didn't argue.

His bed was large and comfortable, and sleeping next to him every night was heaven.

I was falling in love with him.

"Why don't you have central air installed in that old place?" Levi asked one night as we laid naked together in his bed.

"I don't know."

"You should. It isn't cheap, but it's worth it."

"Okay, I can look into it," I told him.

"I know a guy; he'll give you a discount," Levi said as he kissed me.

"Oh, you know a guy, do you?" I teased.

"Yeah, I know a guy," Levi answered as he rolled on top of me, placing himself in between my legs. He brought himself up onto his elbows and looked down at me smiling.

I loved his smile.

"And, what do I have to do to get this discount?"

"Oh," Levi said as he eased his rigid cock into my already wet pussy. "I'm sure we can think of something."

"I'm sure we can," I sighed, moaning as he pulled out and thrust back in, taking his time with me. I was okay with him taking his time.

I fell asleep in Levi's arms, safe and warm and completely satisfied, not wanting this feeling to ever go away.

The next morning, I went home, opening the windows and doors to let in some of the cooler morning air. Levi had left to pick up Rex and head to a job, and I had the day to myself. I planned to use it to revamp my resume and see if any of the local schools were hiring.

After showering and making some coffee, I'd just sat down with my laptop when the sound of a car pulling into my driveway distracted me. Nobody was expected, so I stood up and went to the front door. A bland looking sedan was parked in front of the porch, and an equally bland looking man got out of it. He was holding a large envelope in his hand, and I opened the screen door, greeting him as he came up onto the porch.

"Miss Masters?" he asked.

"That's me. Can I help you?"

"My name is Jim Hartwell, and I am with the state transportation department."

I narrowed my eyes, looking at the man before me. Someone from the state wouldn't be coming here with news I wanted to hear.

"Okay? Can I help you?" I repeated.

"I am here to serve you papers. We were in contact with Polly Nelson almost a year ago regarding this matter, and she turned our offer down. But, it has come to our attention that you are now the legal property owner."

"Yes, I am, but what are you talking about?"

A small, fake, tight smile fell across his face.

"The state is condemning the back end of your property, Miss Masters. We need it to put a highway through. You will be fairly compensated for the property."

I stood there and stared at this man. What in the hell was he talking about?

"No way this can be legal!"

"I assure you it is legal and happens all the time. These documents give you all the details, including the amount we will be paying you. You have two weeks to remove anything from the portion of the property that you want to keep."

"Two weeks?" I cried as I snatched the papers from his hands.

"Yes, there is a map of the property outlining where the cutoff is," he said calmly as he reached out to hand me something else. I took it and saw it was his card.

"Why would I want this? You're already stealing from me. Why the fuck would I want to call you?"

"If you have any questions. I encourage you to have your attorney go over the paperwork."

With that, Jim Hartwell turned around, got in his boring ass car, and left. And I was standing there holding the paperwork that would change everything.

I went to sit at the kitchen table to read over the papers, trying to take in what this all meant. After thirty minutes of mulling, I decided to call Lucy.

"Hey, Lucy," I said when she picked up.

"Hey, there! What's up?" Lucy's voice came through the other end of the phone, as chipper as always.

"Uh, do you know anything about the state wanting the back end of the property?" I asked, trying not to start crying again.

She was quiet for a minute.

"I remember a man came to the house and spoke with us, but Polly turned the offer down. Something about wanting to put a road in?"

"Did he say anything about condemning the land so they could still take it?"

"No," Lucy answered. "What's going on, Evan?"

I tried to calm myself before I spoke again.

"Apparently, the state has other ways to get what they want. I have two weeks to remove anything from the property that I want to keep."

"What?" Lucy's voice mirrored my franticness.

"They are taking it." I started to tear up again.

"Can they really do that?"

"Yes," I replied.

"Call Mr. Hanson, get an appointment today, and let me know what time. I'll meet you there," Lucy instructed me with anger in her voice.

"What about your job? Aren't you working today?"

"Don't worry about me. I can get someone to cover. I'll meet you at the attorney's office," Lucy said and then she hung up.

Two hours later, Lucy and I sat in my aunt's attorney's office as he went over the paperwork Mr. Hartwell had delivered. I sat biting my cuticles until my fingers bled while he read over the documents.

"All of this is legitimate, Evan," he told me as he put the papers down in front of him.

"So, they can really take my property?"

"They can. It's called eminent domain. As long as they are taking the land for public use and they are fairly compensating the landowner, it's legal. They need to put a road in for the new school, that is for the public, and looking over the amount they are going to give you I would say this is more than fair compensation."

"But, what about Aunt Polly's will? I thought the only way I can keep the house is if I remain the owner?" I asked, once again feeling the heat prick the backs of my eyes.

"This doesn't matter, Evan. It's still your home," Mr. Hanson reassured me. "And, looking over the map of where the boundary is, it doesn't look like they are taking more than a couple acres. You won't even notice it."

"I will notice it. The old sycamore sits on the last acre, which means they are going to cut it down."

I thought back to the seventh grade, a year that contradicted everything Mr. Hanson was saying to me.

Seventh grade had gone by so fast. Before I knew it, I found myself back in Kendrick with my aunt and her jerk of a husband. Things seemed different around their house. Something was off; I could feel it.

I had gone over to Della's house the day I arrived, but her mom said she wasn't sure where Della was, but as soon as she got home she would let her know I was there.

I had tried to call Della a few times over the year, but she never answered or called me back. I hoped she was still my friend.

My aunt was as happy as always to see me, and I was thrilled to see her. I adored her, but I still questioned her choice in a husband.

Louis had greeted me when I arrived, trying to hug me, but I was able to get out of it and move around him. He turned to look at me, and I could swear he had a small, evil smile plastered on his thin lips. God, he gave me the creeps so bad. I had made a promise to myself the entire train ride there that I wouldn't let myself be alone with him all summer. It was going to be difficult, but I could do it.

"Do you have any friends who would need a babysitter? I know CPR, and I am really good with kids", I told Aunt Polly the morning after I arrived.

"Oh, I can't think of any right now, but I can ask around," she replied.

I wanted to babysit, make some money, and be out of the house at night when Louis was home. I was sure someone needed to get away from their brats.

Louis hadn't leered at me or tried to touch me in the first week I was there. I hoped what had happened at the tree the previous summer was just a misunderstanding. I did notice how distant he was from Aunt Polly. He seemed irritated with her, and he would snap at her when she would ask him questions. Why would she put up with that? I never saw my aunt as someone weak and to see her letting that douchebag treat her like that made me hate him even more.

"Evan, I think I found you a babysitting job tonight, if you're interested," Aunt Polly announced three weeks into my visit.

I perked up.

"Who?" I asked, excited about making some of my own money.

"Kevin and Alicia, they have a six-year-old girl. Sweetest thing ever. I told them about you, and Alicia called me this morning. It's their anniversary, and they want to go to dinner for a few hours. Are you interested?"

"Yes!" I squealed excitedly.

"Well, they live about a quarter mile down the road, and I told them you would stop over to meet them this afternoon. I knew you would want to, so I already told them yes for you," she confessed, winking at me.

"Thanks, Aunt Polly," I said, kissing her on the cheek. Then, I ran into my room to get ready to go meet with Mrs. Alicia.

A few hours later, I was riding my bike home from meeting with Alicia. She was a super nice lady, and I adored Courtney, her daughter. I was thrilled to have my first babysitting job scheduled for that night.

As I rounded the corner, I saw Della heading into her house.

"Hey, Della!" I called out to her.

She turned and saw me. Then, she turned around and continued into her house. Stopping the bike, I watched as she ignored me, stomping up her front porch stairs and slamming the door shut behind her. I guess that answered my question about us being friends.

*

Babysitting had been a breeze, playing Barbies all night and making boxed macaroni and cheese for dinner. Courtney and I had fun together. She was the easiest kid to watch. I hoped Alicia and Kevin used me for more sitting jobs.

By the time they got home, I had already helped Courtney get ready for bed, putting her in her nightgown and reading her a bedtime story. She was tucked in and ready for her mom and dad to kiss her goodnight.

"How was she?" Kevin asked when they came in.

"She was so good. I think we are best friends now." I laughed as I started to pick up the Barbies scattered all around the living room.

"Don't worry about those. We can do that in the morning," Alicia said as she dug in her purse to pull out her wallet. She grabbed a few bills and handed them to me. I tried not to count them in front of them, but I was sure she handed me fifteen dollars.

"I told Polly we would be home around ten. She said Louis would come get you," Alicia told me.

My smile faded.

"Oh, I could have just walked home. It's not far," I tried to argue, but it was too late. I heard the sound of a vehicle pulling into the gravel driveway. My stomach dropped.

"That's him," Kevin said. "Thank you for watching her. I'm sure we will call you again this summer."

"Okay, thanks," was all I could get out. I walked to the front door and peered out the screen. I saw Aunt Polly's Jeep in the driveway. My legs felt like lead as I walked to the passenger door and opened it to be greeted by the beady eyes of Louis. He smiled at me. I told myself nothing would happen; it was only a five-minute drive down the road.

"Put your seat belt on," Louis told me as I got in. I pulled the belt across me and buckled it. I felt trapped.

The drive started smoothly. He asked me how the night went, and I told him everything went well. He smiled at me and continued to drive at a snail's pace. I watched as the bugs splattered on the windshield, counting them to keep my mind occupied.

The car slowed a little more, and Louis reached over me, rolling my window down. When he brought his hand away, the back of it skimmed across my breasts.

I stiffened up.

"It's nice out tonight," he said, his voice sounding low and menacing to me. He patted my thigh, a gesture that could have been something an uncle would do to his niece, but this uncle left his hand there. I sat still, my eyes not blinking as his hand inched up, stopping just inches from the apex of my thighs.

"I'm glad you're here, Evan. It makes Polly happy. I like to see Polly happy, don't you?" he asked. I just nodded my head, even though I knew he couldn't see me. "I know you do," he murmured quietly as he squeezed my thigh.

We pulled into my aunt's driveway, and as soon as the car was in park, I jumped out, bolting up to the front porch.

"Evan," Louis called out.

I stopped and turned to him. "Yeah?"

"Be quiet when you go in. Polly is already asleep. Just so you know, I'll be the one picking you up from any of your night babysitting jobs. Polly doesn't see so well in the dark," he replied, smiling a smug grin at me.

I didn't answer as I went into the house, stomping up the stairs not caring if I woke my aunt up. When I got to my room, I opened the door and barricaded myself in, pushing my nightstand in front of it.

CHAPTER FIFTEEN

EVAN

I hadn't felt as helpless as I did at that moment in a very long time. I had failed my aunt and was losing part of her beloved property, the part of the property that held a large part of my life. It was just a tree to most people, but to Aunt Polly and me that tree was a symbol of hope. A symbol of our freedom.

I found myself walking the back portion of the land, following the worn path through the tall grass as I made my way to the old tree. It loomed in the distance, tall and proud. It was old. Aunt Polly once told me it was full grown when she was a kid. She loved this place and had bought the land because if it.

And I'd lost it.

As I approached, I saw the rope swing swaying in the slight breeze. It was funny to me how one tree and one rope swing could bring back so many memories, but here it was in person. A forgotten relic of my last two summers in Kendrick. I fucking hated that damn swing.

I walked over to the rope and started yanking on it, trying to break the fragile threads that were unraveling. I kept pulling, putting all of my weight into it, trying to get it down.

"I fucking hate you!" I screamed as I became almost frantic. I wanted that swing down. I didn't know why. I just needed it down.

I worked myself into a sweat as I dug my heels into the soil and threw myself back, holding onto the old, wooden swing. I heard the sound of wood snapping. The next thing I knew, I was on my ass in the dirt with half of the wood in my hands.

I started to cry, holding onto a broken swing and sitting on the ground. I sobbed, the weight of everything coming down on me all at once. My chest felt like someone was standing on it, and I couldn't catch my breath. Laying back, I clutched the wood to my chest and let the tears come. I let everything I had been holding in out and cried like I had never cried before.

I told Levi I wasn't feeling well that night when he texted. He immediately called me.

"What's wrong?" he asked, his voice full of concern.

"I'm just feeling a little under the weather. I think I'm going to take a bath and get in bed. Can I see you tomorrow?"

"Yeah, babe. Of course," Levi told me. "Call me if you need anything tonight. I'll be home."

"Okay, thanks. Talk to you tomorrow."

"Okay, baby doll."

I did not deserve him.

CHAPTER SIXTEEN

LEVI

Something had happened while I was at work, and I knew it. Evan didn't have to tell me. Her voice told me all I needed to hear. I didn't believe for a second she was sick, but she wouldn't lie to me to be deceitful. Something was wrong.

I dialed Lucy to see if she knew anything.

"Hey there, Lucy."

"Hey, Levi. What's up?" she asked, her voice as cheery as ever.

"I was wondering if you knew what was going on with Evan. She said she wasn't feeling good, but her voice seemed off."

"Oh." Her voice changed from cheerful to cautious in a second.

"What, Lucy? You know something. Spill it, girl."

"Well," Lucy started, clearing her throat. "Uh, Evan was served with papers today. The state is taking the back part of the land to put a road through. She's really upset about it."

What the fuck? Why would Evan keep something like that from me?

"I'm sure she is. Okay, thanks, Lucy. I'll talk to you soon."

"Don't tell her I told you!" Lucy cried out before I hung up.

"Look, once the state comes in, this ain't going to be a secret. It won't matter who told me when that happens, so why does it matter now?"

She didn't answer.

"I got to go. Talk to you later," was all I said before I hung up.

I ran across the road to Evan's, stomping up the front steps and knocking on the door. She didn't answer. I pounded on the door once more and still no answer, so I tried the knob on the door, and it turned.

Walking into the house, I called her name but got no answer. Her car was there, and it was too dark out for her to be wandering the property, so I climbed the steps to go to her bedroom. Looking in there, I found it empty. Then, I remembered she was going to take a bath.

I quietly opened the door to the bathroom and found her soaking in the old claw foot tub. Her eyes were closed, head back, and she had headphones in which explained why she didn't hear me calling. I would need to have a fucking talk with her about locking the damn front door.

I took in the sight of a wet, naked Evan in the bath. The steam from the water swirled around her, and the vision was so fucking erotic that my dick started to get hard just watching her.

The tub was deep, but I could see her tits bobbing just under the surface of the water. Fuck, she was sexy. Her hair was piled on top of her head, and her face was makeup free, giving her the appearance of a young girl, rather than a thirty-one-year-old woman.

I stood over her, just watching. When her eyes opened, she nearly jumped right out of the tub.

"Holy shit!" she shouted, grabbing her chest as if she was having a heart attack.

"Serves you right," I scolded. "What the fuck are you thinking not locking your front door when you're up here and can't hear when someone is yelling your fucking name? I could have been an axe murderer or something."

"I doubt an axe murderer wants to come all the way down this road to kill me," she mocked.

"Doesn't matter. You lock the damn door at night from now on," I replied as I kneeled down next to the tub. Looking at her, I could see she had been crying.

"Why've you been crying, baby?" I asked.

"I take it you already know, or you wouldn't be here."

"I want you to tell me, not hear it from someone else. Why didn't you think you could tell me?"

"It wasn't that I couldn't. I didn't want to. Not yet. I'm still processing all of it."

Looking at her, I could see just how fucking lost she was, and it gutted me.

"I'm right here for you, baby doll. You don't need to process this alone. I see this shit all the time, hell, sometimes I'm the guy who tears someone's land apart for the state."

"That doesn't make me feel better." She scowled.

"It doesn't fucking matter. It's not going to change, so just put your big girl panties on and move on. How much land are they taking?" I asked.

"The back of the property, about two acres."

"Two acres is nothing. You'll still have twelve, you can't even see to the back of the property, so you won't notice it."

"What are you talking about? How will I not notice that big ass tree that has been there forever is no longer sitting there?"

I hadn't thought of the old sycamore that edged the last portion of the land. The thing had to be almost two hundred years old.

"I don't know what to say, Evan."

Really, there was nothing to say. That tree meant something to her, but there was no stopping what was already in motion.

"Me either," she said as she slid further into the water until she was up to her chin. She looked at me and gave a small smile. I leaned over and took her face in my hands.

"Everything will be fine," I promised her as I leaned in further to brush a light kiss on her plump lips, lips I couldn't get enough of. I parted them with my tongue, deepening the kiss. She moaned into my mouth, and that was the only trigger I needed. I slowly slid my arm into the water, finding her folds, circling her throbbing clit. Evan pulled away from the kiss as she threw her head back, taking a deep intake of breath, only to let it out as she came undone. Those fucking sounds coming from her mouth were almost enough to make me come in my damn pants. As she lay back in the tub, I watched as she let me bring her to orgasm. I loved how responsive she was, how she moaned and sighed when my hands found the spots that needed to be touched.

I slid a finger in her pussy, working it in and out of her as the water from the tub sloshed over the sides. Evan began to wail as her orgasm took over. I pumped faster, watching her face as she climaxed.

She was fucking gorgeous.

"Stand up," I commanded. Her eyes opened to find me standing over the tub, unzipping my jeans and pulling my hard cock free. I started stroking myself. "Stand up," I repeated, keeping my eyes trained on hers.

She watched me jerk off.

She stood, her skin pink from the hot water. I reached my free hand out for her to take as she stepped out of the tub.

"What..." she began, but I pulled her to me and kissed her, quieting her questions. Turning our bodies, I walked her backwards until her ass hit the bathroom counter. I pulled back and looked at her. Her eyes were hooded, her lips swollen, and her nipples hard.

Fuck yes.

In one swift motion, I turned her body and bent her over the counter, lining my cock up with her hot pussy and entering her in one hard thrust. A deep moan came from Evan, and I thrust hard, again and again, watching her in the mirror. She was watching me as I fucked her, and it was so fucking sexy. I looked down as I pumped my cock in and out of her, watching as I withdrew and slammed back in. My cock was coated with her juices, and the sounds of skin slapping skin, moaning, and wet fucking were all there was in that bathroom.

Evan placed her hands on the mirror, bracing herself as I continued to relentlessly fuck her, her entire body rocking forward with each thrust. It was raw and dirty, not a hint of tenderness, but she was so fucking into it that I knew I wasn't going to last much longer. I looked up to find her still watching me, and I smirked. Pulling out, I came all over her ass, never taking my eyes off hers.

CHAPTER SEVENTEEN

EVAN

Levi stayed with me, sleeping in my bed and not saying anything about the tears that fell from my tired eyes. I didn't know how to tell him the tree was so much more for me than just an old tree. That it held something that changed my life.

I was so in love with him, something I thought I would never find. Another thing I didn't know how to tell him, but I needed to. But, how do you tell the man you love you fucked almost every man in the previous town you lived in? Fucked them for the attention and momentary intimacy they provided? How would I tell him my life has been shit all by my own doing? I hid it well, plastering a fake smile and a fake personality for people during the day. But at night? At night, I let the demons that haunted me take over, trapping me within my own thoughts. Thoughts that I was trash, dirty, and not worth loving. I didn't think I deserved Levi, but there was something there. Something about him that told me he once had his own demons and maybe he still did. Something that told me I could trust him with my darkest secret, the one that controlled my entire life.

I was so fucking scared.

The following day I was out at the tree, laying on the ground watching the sky when I heard footsteps.

Levi.

I sat up and smiled when I saw him walking toward me. He carried a blanket and two beers.

"Hey there, baby doll," he greeted as he handed me the beers so he could lay the blanket out.

"Hey, how was work?"

"Hot and filthy."

He was dressed in an old gray T-shirt with a pair of camo shorts. He wasn't much of a fashion statement, but I had never seen him in anything I didn't want to rip off of him.

We sat in silence, drinking our beers and being together. He never filled the air with mindless chatter, something I appreciated. I just liked being near him.

"I love you, Evan," he said after a few more minutes of quiet.

I closed my eyes and smiled, looking up to the sky as I silently thanked Aunt Polly for bringing me to this man. She knew exactly what she had been doing.

I let out a heavy breath.

"I love you, too."

"I know you do, baby, I know. And that's why I need you to tell me what the fuck is going on."

I looked at him, the smile falling from my face. This wasn't how I envisioned the first time I told him I loved him.

"What do you mean?" I questioned, confused at what he wanted.

"This tree, it's something more to you than I know, isn't it?"

I felt my heart stop in my chest.

"What happened to the rope swing?" Levi asked, eyeing where the shredded rope swayed.

"I tore it down."

"Why?"

I didn't answer.

"Evan, look at me, damn it," Levi commanded.

I brought my eyes to his and instantly felt the burn of tears.

He knew something.

"What did she tell you?"

"How about if you tell me? I'm tired of hearing everything about your life second hand."

Oh fuck, could I tell him everything?

And then, it hit me.

Yes, I could.

I needed to.

And, so I began.

I babysat for Alicia and Kevin on a warm afternoon. They wanted to drive into Philadelphia and go to a baseball game, so I sat with Courtney. We had a great day running through the sprinkler and eating popsicles all day. She was the sweetest little girl. I hoped one day I had a daughter just like her.

I brought her in and gave her a bath, cleaning the day's grime and popsicle dye from her face. She splashed and played in the cool bath while I got out her nightgown. Once she was dressed, I braided her long hair, and we sat downstairs watching her favorite movie, The Little Mermaid. She treated me to a full concert, singing along with all the songs. I just laughed, clapping along with the music.

Her parents arrived home a little before eight. It was still light enough out that I was able to convince them I was okay walking home.

"How about you at least call us when you get there, okay?" Alicia made me promise.

"I will."

I walked home, staying to the right side of the road kicking gravel as I went. I passed nothing but field. The sounds of the crickets and the locusts were so loud that I could barely hear the gravel crunching under my feet. I loved that sound. To me, this was home, not the subdivision I lived in with my mother in our three-bedroom ranch home. My mom was great; she tried so hard but, in the end, her career came before me. She loved me, but I needed the love and affection a mom was supposed to give. The love and affection Aunt Polly gave me. If she hadn't married Louis, I would have wanted to live with her.

When I got home, I found a note on the counter from Aunt Polly. She had gone to play Bunco, and Louis was working late. I had the house to myself.

After I called Alicia to let her know I got home okay, I went upstairs and ran a bath in the old claw foot tub I loved so much. I brought in my book, panties, and light summer nightgown Aunt Polly had bought for me. It was white with little pink flowers on it and came to my knees. The fabric was so soft and light; it was perfect for sleeping on the hot nights.

I slipped into the tub, washing my hair and face before getting out My Sweet Audrina and reading. The water was cool and felt good on my overheated skin. The evenings were just as warm and muggy as the days, so my nightly showers were always with cooler water. My bath wouldn't be different.

I sat in there for what could have been hours, reading until my skin was pruned up. I got out and towel dried myself, stepping over to the bathroom counter and finding the bottle of Jergens lotion I had asked for. I slathered it over my skin until I felt silky smooth. I pulled my hair into a braid and brushed my teeth before I went into my room for the night.

Looking out my window, I saw that neither Louis nor Aunt Polly was home yet, so I sat on top of my covers, propping my pillows up so I could keep reading until I fell asleep.

I woke up sometime later, noticing the light in my room had been turned off. I sat up and looked around the now darkened room and realized I was not alone. I could make out Louis standing in front of my closed door.

I froze.

He had the front of his pants open and his hand wrapped around his penis.

"Shhhhh..." was all he said as he walked over and sat on the edge of my bed, looking at me as he still gripped himself, working his hand back and forth. I could smell the alcohol seeping out of his pores. He was drunk.

"You need to leave," I demanded, trying to move back on the bed. He grabbed my ankle and yanked, pulling me closer to him.

"You need to watch your smart mouth, girl."

His hand snaked up my thigh, under my nightgown, and brushed along the crotch of my panties. I bit back a cry, trying to remain calm and collected. I moved back, pushing his hand away.

"Get out!" I shouted, pointing my hand at the door. I was trapped, his large body blocking the direct route to the door. My bed was in the corner of the room, right under the window, and I had a quick flash of an idea to climb out of it.

Louis had other ideas. He gripped both of my calves and yanked me down. I cried out in pain and began thrashing around as he pinned me with his weight.

"Now, you listen here," he hissed, his rank breath in my face as his hand fumbled under my nightgown. "You've been prancing around this house in this little number for days now, making my dick hard. You know what you're doing, you little slut."

I felt his hand on my crotch, pulling my underwear to the side as he pushed a finger in me. I cried out.

"NO!" I screamed as I began to kick and hit, trying to grab onto anything to hit him with.

"Shut up!" he roared as I felt him move closer to me, pushing my nightgown up around my hips.

"NO. NO. NO!"

I felt searing pain between my legs, Louis grunting as he tore through my body. This couldn't be happening. I punched at his back as he grunted again, spittle hitting my face as he hurt me over and over.

"NO!" I continued to scream, but he didn't hear me.

The door smashed against the wall, and I heard Aunt Polly.

"What in the hell are you doing?" she screamed out, running forward and hitting Louis with closed fists. He didn't have time to react as Aunt Polly reached for his gun, pulling it free from the holster and taking aim.

Louis climbed off of me and turned to her.

"She invited me in here," he lied, slurring his words as he tried to tuck himself back in his pants.

"Like hell she did! I could hear her all the way outside! You raped my niece, you son of a bitch!"

Louis rushed forward, and that's when it happened. A loud popping noise went off, and Louis crumbled to the ground. Two more pops and he didn't get up.

Aunt Polly had shot him.

And killed him.

I sat there, tears uncontrollably spilling from my eyes, shaking. I looked down in between my legs and cried out when I saw the blood on my panties and nightgown.

Aunt Polly rushed over to me, pulling me into her arms, and cried with me. I held tightly to her as she rocked me back and forth.

After a few minutes, she pulled back.

"Evan, look at me. Are you okay?"

I shook my head. I was most certainly not okay.

"Okay, sweetie. Okay. I promise everything will be okay." It sounded like she was telling this to herself more than to me.

"I need you to help me, honey."

"Help you what?" I asked, my teeth chattering.

"I need to get rid of him, and I think I have a plan."

After setting her plan in motion, Aunt Polly helped me into the shower, throwing away my ruined night clothes. I stood in the shower crying, the ache between my thighs not letting me forget the nightmare I had just been put through. When I got out, she had laid *out a pair of sleep shorts and an old T-shirt. I put them on and found her in my room with Louis wrapped in a tarp.*

"What are you doing?"

"This bastard was going to leave me for a woman he was talking to in one of those chat rooms on the internet. So, that is exactly what he's doing. Leaving."

"Why don't we just call the police?"

"Because this looks real bad. I just shot and killed the sheriff."

"Because he was hurting me!"

"This wasn't self-defense. This was a crime of anger. But, I think we can pull this off. Now, are you with me?" she asked.

I nodded my head, not knowing what else to do.

"Help me get him outside. I pulled the tractor around, and we are going to get him in the bucket."

We dragged the tarp down the stairs, the thudding sounds with every step making my stomach turn. Getting him through the kitchen and out the back door, I saw Aunt Polly's orange tractor sitting there. The bucket was placed on the ground, so we rolled the tarp into it.

"Okay, now we need to get upstairs and clean the room."

She was beginning to scare me. She seemed a little too comfortable with the disposal and clean-up of a murder.

In the kitchen, she mixed up a concoction of dish soap, bleach, vinegar and baking soda in a large bucket. Grabbing towels and sponges, she ushered me back up the stairs, and we began to clean the blood. I was surprised there wasn't much.

"Shouldn't there be more blood?" I asked as I rinsed my sponge and began to scrub again.

"Only one bullet exited the body, and he fell backwards. His clothes are bloody, but we mostly have blood splatter."

I stopped and looked at her.

"I watch Forensic Files. I learn a lot," she told me.

When we were done, the room looked cleaner than when we had started. Aunt Polly took the towels, sponges, and bucket and brought them outside, placing them in the bucket with Louis.

She then went back inside and began to gather up his belongings.

"What are you doing?"

"Making him leave like I said."

She got all of his clothes and toiletries, the things he would take with him on a trip.

"Evan, go find a suitcase for me, please." Her voice was calm.

She kept her luggage in the attic, so I went down the hall to the door that led up to the third story. It had originally been used as more bedrooms when the house was first built but was turned into attic space when the house had been remodeled some years back.

It was hot up there. I found the light dangling from the ceiling and pulled the cord, turning it on. It illuminated the space with harsh light, and I had to squint to get used to its brightness.

I looked in each room of the attic until I found a large, brown fake leather suitcase. I pulled it out of the back of the room where it was wedged in behind boxes marked 'board games' and quickly left the room. I turned the light off and came back down the stairs and into the kitchen where Aunt Polly was just hanging up the phone.

"Who were you calling?" I panicked. I didn't want her to tell my mom.

"A friend. Someone I trust. He's going to help us out."

"You have a friend who is going to help you cover up killing someone?"

"Not exactly, but he can make all of Louis's things go away. You and I are going to cover up the killing part."

I felt myself beginning to cry.

Aunt Polly came over and pulled me into her arms, hugging me tightly.

"Listen to me," she said as I sniffled into her shirt. "If I hadn't come home early, who knows what else would have happened? I am just thankful I did. And, I don't regret what I did, not at all. Do you understand?"

She didn't regret shooting and killing her husband.

I was happy she did it.

That wasn't what I was crying about. I was crying about what he did to me. What he took from me. Something I could never ever get back. Something I had valued and wanted to wait until marriage to give away.

I was happy she had shot and killed that bastard.

He would never be able to do it again.

We put the suitcase in Louis's sheriff's car. The smell of his cheap cologne was stagnant in the confined space. The smell made my stomach turn, and I leaned over, vomiting. The night's events hit me again, and I felt the burn rise in my throat once more, expelling nothing but stomach acid.

I stayed leaned over, my hands on my knees as Aunt Polly rubbed my back. Catching my breath, I wiped my mouth clean and stood up.

"I'm okay," I lied.

"You're not, but you will be," she said, her voice filled with something I thought might be guilt.

We drove the tractor to the edge of the property, near the old sycamore tree. She wanted him far enough away from the house that she wouldn't need to think about him, but close enough that she could keep an eye on him.

She stopped some distance from the tree, near the fence line and lowered the bucket, dropping the body on the ground. I climbed off the back and stood under the tree with the spotlight we had brought to use as our headlight. No one was around to question the light so late at night, the neighbor behind her having his home some fifteen acres away.

I watched as she dug a large hole, the bucket filling with dirt and rock and being dumped on the ground in a loud whoosh.

Once the hole looked to be almost six-feet deep, Aunt Polly hopped down from the seat. She waved me over, and together we rolled the tarp into the hole. She quickly climbed back into the seat and began catching the dirt she dug up in the bucket, pouring it into the hole. Once most of the dirt was put back, she patted it down with the bucket. It was obvious a hole had been dug, but no one but us ever came out here, so who would ever question it?

We rode back to the house in silence, neither of us saying a word about what we'd just done. When we pulled the tractor into the *small barn and came out, I saw that Louis's car was gone. I looked at my aunt.*

"No one will ever see that again," was all she said.

That night and every night after, I slept in my aunt's room, where I had someone to comfort me when I woke up in a sweat from the nightmares that plagued my sleep.

A week later, Aunt Polly drove me three towns over to a woman's clinic where they gave me a pregnancy test and tested me for sexually transmitted diseases. I was grateful when everything came back clear. When my aunt had told the doctor I had been raped, they gave me the number for a counselor to talk to.

Talking with the women's crisis counselor didn't help as much as I wanted it to. She reminded me I had not asked for what happened and the only way to not let my rapist win was to take back my life and keep living. She gave me literature to read about surviving rape and methods to help cope and sent me on my way as if being raped was the most normal thing in the world. I doubted she had ever been raped.

Aunt Polly had asked around town about Louis, claiming she came home from Bunco and he was gone. I backed up her story saying he wasn't there when I got home from babysitting, and I hadn't seen him.

Aunt Polly had been on to him about his chat room activities. And, when she asked at the sheriff's office, one of the deputies followed us out to the parking lot to talk to us.

"I don't know how to tell you this, Polly, but Louis was talking to some woman from Arizona over one of those chat rooms," the young deputy said.

"I know all about her. What's her name? Cynthia, that's right. I know all about Cynthia. He isn't very good at hiding his chat room history," Aunt Polly said, playing it up.

"He planned on leaving you for her, Polly."

Aunt Polly stood there and looked at the deputy. He looked away, uncomfortable with the glare my aunt was raining down on him.

"Good riddance. I hope they are very happy together," she spat, turning on her heels and walking to her Jeep.

I smiled at the deputy and ran after her, getting in the passenger side and shutting the door behind me. She drove off, squealing the tires as she left the parking lot.

"And now, we will never speak of Louis again, understand? That piece of shit doesn't deserve to take up any more of our thoughts."

CHAPTER EIGHTEEN

EVAN

I couldn't look at Levi when I was done telling him about Louis. I was scared to see the look of disgust on his face. Fresh tears fell as I relived the details of the night that forever changed the events of my life.

Warm hands gripped me, pulling me to him, and he engulfed me in love. Love I never thought I would have.

Love I needed.

Love I wanted.

He pulled back and looked me in the eyes, the look on his face not showing a hint of disgust.

"This explains so much," Levi told me.

"What?" I asked, wiping the tears from my face.

"Polly told me she killed her husband, but I wasn't sure she knew what she was saying."

"What? When did she tell you that?"

"A couple months before you got here. She told me she caught him with another woman and shot his sorry ass."

"And, you didn't think she knew what she was saying?"

"I had a feeling she was telling the truth. There was something in the way she said it. Like she was remembering and not imagining," Levi told me. "She didn't give too many details, though, and now I know why."

Because the details were too horrific.

"And, now that you know she wasn't making it up, what do you think?"

Levi took my face in his hands and looked at me, searching my face.

"Evan, I think that pedophile, rapist fuck got what he deserved. I always knew Polly was one amazing woman, but now she is on my short list of heroes. You shouldn't feel one ounce of regret for what happened to him after he put his fucking hands on you. You were a little fucking girl," Levi said, never taking his eyes off me. "Polly did what was right."

The years of my life after that night were always filled with darkness, a darkness I let engulf me. A darkness that seemed to be brightening ever since I met Levi.

"You aren't disgusted by me?" I whispered.

"Why would I be? You didn't deserve what happened, and if he was still alive, I would fucking kill him myself."

The relief that washed over me hit me like a tidal wave. I let out a breath I hadn't realized I was holding in.

"She did tell me a few things though," Levi continued.

I snapped my attention back to him.

"What did she tell you?"

"She told me about getting rid of his things," Levi began. "Do you know why she told me that?"

I shook my head.

Levi smiled. "Because it was my Uncle Mack that she called."

"What? Seriously? He was the guy she knew?"

"Yep, Mack had some shady fucking connections. He was the one who got my parole officer to stop checking in."

Wait.

What?

"Parole officer?" Levi hadn't told me anything about being in prison.

"You once said we have a lot in common, and you're right, we do."

Swallowing, I asked, "What kind of things in common?"

"Do you know how I know Sheriff Cash?" Levi asked, sitting back on the blanket and resting his weight on his elbows.

I turned to face him, pulling my knees to my chest and resting my head on them.

"Old friends?" I guessed.

"Not exactly."

CHAPTER NINETEEN

LEVI

My past had a strange way of following me around. First, I had Brendan who made sure I ended up in a town where he could keep tabs on me. Then, it was Polly who had known my uncle and turned to him to help her and her niece hide the monster who deserved to be shot and killed.

And then, there was Evan.

"Yes, I had a parole officer."

"What did you do?" she asked.

"Do you want the story or the real story?"

She said nothing as her eyes widened and a small smile appeared on her lips.

"Did you lie about something bad, Levi?"

"A little," I confessed. "I was fifteen and coming home from baseball practice," I began, digging up old memories I tried to keep in my past.

The ride home from baseball practice took me thirty minutes every day. While I watched my friends get picked up from the field by their moms, I packed up my gear and always rode my bike. My mom didn't even know I played baseball. She was too busy drinking her life away and getting beat up by her loser boyfriend, Dean. I fucking hated that guy.

Dean had been with my mom for three years. The first few months, he came across as a nice guy. Once we moved into his three-bedroom, shitty ranch home, things changed. He started to yell at my mom, who was more than used to the abusive boyfriend thing. The last five of them were all abusive. She had a type. Losers.

Dean not only yelled at her, but he kept the physical stuff behind closed doors. At first.

The first time I saw him hurt her I was thirteen. He had just got home from work, and when he opened the refrigerator and found it empty of beer, he called my mom into the kitchen.

"Open that fridge, Candy," he demanded, a sneer spread across his face.

I watched with wide eyes as my mom did as he told her. She looked in and looked back to him.

"Okay," she said, confused.

"Just what is missing from there?"

"Um, I don't know, what?" she asked.

"My fucking beer!" he roared, advancing on my mom and grabbing her upper arm. "Why the fuck is there no beer?"

"You drank it last night," she cried.

"So, why didn't you go to the store and get more?"

"I don't have a car! You're hurting me!"

Dean threw her to the ground, kicking her in the back as he walked by her.

"Fucking worthless bitch," he spat, grabbing his keys and heading out the door.

I went over to my mom, kneeling down beside her.

"Mom, are you okay?" I asked, scared as I watched her roll around in pain.

"Get away from me!" she screamed when I touched her.

I backed away from her and watched as she stayed in the fetal position, lying next to the open fridge door.

That was the last time I ever tried to help my mom when Dean beat her.

But, Dean got bored of only beating my mom and started raising his hands to me. I was small for my age and an easy target, so fighting back wasn't much of an option.

I went to school with bruises on my arms, black eyes, and swollen cheekbones on more than one occasion. No one said a word about it.

But, the summer I turned fourteen I began to fill out. I grew five inches and gained almost twenty pounds, and Dean's beatings became less frequent.

At least, his beatings on me did.

My mom had become one of those women you would see that you felt disgusted by. Her once pretty face was gaunt, and her skin seemed too big for her frame. She was missing one of her front teeth, courtesy of Dean, and her hair was thin and dull.

She looked every bit the part of the dirty alcoholic and drug addict she had become. I wasn't sure what she was snorting up her nose and smoking in the garage, but it was filthy. She smelled bad and had open sores on her skin.

She didn't give a shit about me or what I did.

Our neighbor, Mr. Jensen, was an older man, and he was a huge Philly's fan. I would go over to his place, and we would throw the baseball around. I was sure he knew my home life was less than healthy.

"Hey kid," Mr. Jensen called out to me one January afternoon on my walk home from school. I turned to watch him come down his front porch with papers in his hand.

"Hey there, Mr. Jensen. What's up?"

"I got you something today, and I think you should sign up for it."

He handed me the paperwork, and I looked at it. Recreational baseball registration. I looked from the paperwork to Mr. Jensen.

"Baseball?" I asked, a little excited about the possibility.

"Sure, a kid your age should be doing something for the summer; why not baseball?"

I looked over the paperwork and saw there was a twenty-five dollar sign up fee. I shook my head.

"Thanks, but I don't think my mom will give me the money for the fees."

Mr. Jensen put his hand on my shoulder and squeezed.

"Why do you think I want to see you play baseball? To get you out of that house. Don't you worry about the fees. I will pay for those."

The kind gesture almost made me cry. I couldn't remember the last time someone had done something so nice for me. The clothes on my back came from donation boxes, and our food I got from the local food bank.

I took care of myself.

"I don't want to hear anything but thank you," Mr. Jensen told me.

"Thank you, Mr. Jensen."

*

I played baseball that summer, making a few friends on the team and setting myself up with carpools for away games. Sometimes, Mr. Jensen would take me, cheering loudly for me in the stands.

Neither my mom nor Dean knew where I was going every day. Nor did they give a shit.

When Mr. Jensen passed away the following winter of a heart attack, my heart broke. He had been the only person in my life who really cared about me, the closest thing to a parent I would ever have.

I continued to play baseball, doing chores and yard work for people around the neighborhood to make the money I would need for the fees that spring. I made enough money that after fees were paid I was able to buy an old Mongoose BMX bike from one of my teammates to get back and forth to the fields.

The coaches were all happy to see me, and I was once again able to find rides for away games.

I was away from my house as much as possible.

But not enough.

Most days, I rode home from practice, taking my time to avoid being at the house that was supposed to be my home.

It was anything but a home.

It was a fucking prison.

Riding onto the lawn one day, I dropped my bike, slung my bag over my shoulder and headed up the porch. The house was strangely quiet.

No TV.

No yelling.

Nothing.

Opening the door, the smell of cigarettes and mildew hit my senses.

And something else.

A musty, metallic smell was in the air. A smell you didn't have to be a genius to recognize.

The smell of blood.

I saw Dean sitting on the couch, a bottle in one hand and a smoke in the other. He looked up at me with a wild look in his eyes.

"There you are, you little fuck," he slurred, putting the cigarette to his lips and taking a long drag. He stood up, coming to stand in front of me, and blew the smoke in my face.

I refused to blink.

"Your mom had a bad fucking day," he sneered, turning to look behind him. I followed his gaze to see my mom heaped on the floor, her head a matted mess of blood.

"I think you're about to have one, too, you little piece of fucking shit."

He lunged for me, but I was able to duck under his arm. I ran to my mom, dropping the bag with all my gear on the floor.

"Mom!" I yelled, shaking her limp body.

"Good luck. You can't wake a dead whore."

I saw red, nothing but red as I slid the second-hand baseball bat I had been given out of my bag. Standing, I started to walk towards the man who'd killed my mother.

"What'dya think you're gonna do with that? You ain't got the balls," Dean taunted.

"All I need is this bat," I replied as I swung, hitting him in the side. He doubled over, clutching his ribs, and I swung again, hitting him on the other side.

He yelled out, but I didn't fucking care. I swung my bat again, hitting him in the back, causing him to fall face first onto the floor.

"Jesus fucking Christ, kid!" he wheezed out, his voice garbled, most likely from a punctured lung.

I didn't see him as a person anymore but as a target. A target I had every intention of eliminating.

Walking around him, he looked up, and I saw fear in his eyes.

His fear fed my thirst to end his pathetic fucking life.

His fear mirrored the fear I had lived in for years under his thumb.

His fear made my heart race and my blood pump.

I stood over him, smiling at him the way he had smiled at me so many times. Like a sadist fuck.

"I think it's time you meet Jesus fucking Christ," I told him, right before I brought the bat down one last time on the back of his skull.

A dull thud sounded, and I felt as the bat pierced through his skull as it gave way.

I had no remorse as I watched his body go limp.

I felt a heavy weight lift off my shoulders.

In a haze, I went to the kitchen and dialed for help. I gave the man on the other end my address. Within minutes, a patrol car was in my driveway, a young police officer at my door.

"I'm officer Cash. Someone called 9-1-1 from this number?", he asked when I opened the door.

"That was me," I responded, opening the door wider. I saw his eyes widen as he took in the scene behind me.

"Uh, what happened?" the officer asked as he stepped inside, shutting the door behind him.

I said nothing.

The officer looked at me, studying my reaction, but I was calm. He went back to the murder scene in front of him. He said nothing for a few minutes.

"Levi, right?"

That got my attention.

I hadn't given anyone my name.

"Yeah," I replied, not giving him anything else.

Officer Cash was quiet once more, studying the bodies while he was deep in thought.

"Was your mom dead when you got here?" he asked.

I nodded, looking away.

"And then, Dean Lockwood attacked you and forced you to act in self-defense, right?"

My eyes snapped back to his.

"What?" I whispered.

"That's what happened, right?" he repeated.

I realized he was coaching me.

"Yeah, yeah that's what happened."

Officer Cash nodded as he got on his radio, calling for an ambulance and another officer. Once the voice on the other end confirmed the address, he put the radio back to his shoulder and came over to me.

"Look," he said, grabbing my attention once again. "Dean Lockwood is a low life that no one is going to miss. I know the shit that has gone down in this place, and I know you're a good kid. It may not have been self-defense today, but it was self-defense. I will do everything I can to help you, but you have to do what I tell you. Got it?"

That one statement told me Officer Cash was going to be part of my world for the rest of my life.

*

I ended up getting three years in the Shuman Juvenile Detention Center for involuntary manslaughter charges. Turns out, I swung that bat a few too many times.

I kept my head down there, concentrating on my schooling and taking advantage of the programs they offered.

I wasn't going to end up like my mom.

I made no friends, and I only spoke to people enough to get me through. No one fucked with me once they found out the reason I was there.

Turns out, most of the punk kids in the place were there for drugs or theft.

No one wanted to mess with the guy who killed someone.

143

I was released into the care of my uncle, and I was given five years probation. Probation I was to serve while living in Kendrick learning a trade.

About a month after I moved in with my uncle, Officer Cash paid me a visit. His uniform was different, and so was his title.

"Good to see you, Levi," he said when I came to the screen door. His smile was genuine.

"You too, Officer Cash."

"It's Sheriff Cash, now."

"Oh. Sheriff of Kendrick?" I asked.

He nodded. "Yep. I just wanted to come by and welcome one of our newest residents. You stay out of trouble, Mr. Kinkaid. Got it?"

Smiling, I nodded. "Yes, sir. That's the plan."

CHAPTER TWENTY

EVAN

I sat there, watching Levi.

He had killed someone.

He had lied about it.

He had gotten away with it.

Just like I had.

"We have a lot in common," he said, smiling at me.

"We do," I agreed, my heart racing from what he had just told me.

Levi and I were victims of unthinkable acts brought to us by people that, in a perfect world, we should have been able to trust. People who should have been among the adults who protected us. Instead, they'd hurt us. They had ruined us.

The difference between Levi and me?

He overcame his past and used it to free himself.

I never overcame mine and had been trapped within my own darkness because of it.

"So, Brendan helped you?" I asked.

"Yeah, he did. He's all for staying on the right side of the law, but he also has no issues making certain people go away. People no one will miss."

"So, he's a dirty cop?"

"Kind of, in the best possible way. He doesn't always agree with our justice system. So, he makes his own. People around here aren't dumb, they know. But, no one cares because he keeps the town clean, or at least cleaner."

I thought about meeting Sheriff Brendan Cash. He came across as such a friendly man, one who I would have never guessed as someone who would help cover up a murder.

"He's a great guy, Evan," Levi stated, obviously feeling the need to defend the sheriff.

I smiled. "I agree."

Levi sat forward, taking my hands in his.

"I told you about all of this for a couple reasons. One is I don't want any fucking secrets between us," he said, his gaze serious and commanding.

"What's the other reason?" I asked.

Levi was quiet for a minute, carefully choosing his words.

"The other is because I am going to need some help on this. I'll need help helping you."

Help helping me?

"What's that mean?" I questioned.

"You have a dead fucking body somewhere around here, right? The state is coming in within the next week or so to start digging up the land to put a road through. I think it would be a wise idea to get that body out of its homemade grave, don't you?"

Oh. That.

"Probably," I agreed. "Who will help you?"

"Rex and Brendan," Levi answered like the three of them dug up old corpses and disposed of them all the time.

"What will you do with it?"

Levi leaned over, planting a kiss on my lips.

"How about this? The less you know about what we do with it, the better," he suggested.

I thought it was a great idea.

CHAPTER TWENTY-ONE

LEVI

"So, let me get this right," Rex said, taking a swig of beer as we sat on my front porch. "Evan, that fine piece of ass across the road, helped Polly, the sweetest woman who ever lived, murder and dispose of a child rapist?"

"Yep," I replied, taking a drink from my own beer and watching the farmhouse across the road.

It had been a few days since Evan and I told each other about our pasts.

A few days since I told her I loved her.

And she loved me back.

"So, when are we digging and ditching the rotten cock sucker?"

Leave it to Rex, he was one man I could always count on regardless of the circumstances.

"We got to do this shit soon," I told him. "We've only got about a week before they break ground back there, and I don't even know exactly where he is."

"I can't believe Polly has kept this for nineteen fucking years. She was a fucking criminal mastermind." Rex laughed as he put his empty bottle back in the case and grabbed a full one, popping the top and flicking it at me.

He was right. The fact that Polly kept this covered up for so long was nothing short of a fucking miracle. The story

148

she used was a weak one. Who would vanish in the middle of the night never to be heard from and no one question it?

A worthless piece of shit that hurt little girls.

"I'm going to have Brendan help on some of the backstory," I told Rex. "I know he has a few tech guys who owe him some favors. I think I can get him to call a couple in."

"Fuck Cash, man. That guy's a fuckwad."

Rex wasn't a big fan of our town sheriff, probably because he had been arrested by him multiple times.

Brendan didn't give a shit who Rex was or who he was friends with, if he got out of line and fucked up, he got arrested.

Most recently, Rex was in the back of Brendan's car for being drunk and disorderly and indecent exposure. That arrest was made when Rex was walking down the sidewalk after a night at Andy's with his cock out pissing all over as he went. It took ten minutes for Brendan to get Rex to tuck it in. He spent the night in a jail cell, and in the morning, I got a call asking me to come down and get my friend. No charges were ever filed, but Rex's hatred for the sheriff remained strong.

"That fuckwad has kept your ass from serving actual time on more than one occasion. You do fucking realize some of the shit he has got you for could have been the real fucking deal, right? Like months behind bars?" I reminded him.

Rex shook his head, scratching his bushy as hell beard. "I don't fucking care. He's still a fuckwad."

*

That night, I drove my truck over to Evan's. The air was warm, and as the sun began to set, the fireflies came out in full force.

It was the perfect setting for what I needed to do.

What we needed to do.

Parking next to her Subaru, I got out and walked up the steps, knocking on the screen door. I checked it before she saw me, making sure it was locked.

It was.

That's my girl.

"Hey," Evan said as she unlocked the door, swinging it open for me. I grabbed hold of her and pulled her lush body to me. I fucking loved her body; her curves were enough to bring a man to his knees.

"Get some shoes on," I said, still holding her against me.

"Again with the caveman act," she teased.

"Baby, it's no act. Now, go get some shoes on."

I released her and watched as she slid her feet into a pair of old flip flops.

"Let's go," I motioned for her to head out the front door to my waiting truck. Surprisingly, she did without an argument. I turned and followed, locking the door behind us.

She sat in the middle of my bench seat, my hand on her thigh as we drove to the back of her property.

"What are we doing?" she asked, hesitance in her voice.

"You'll see."

"What's with all the cryptic stuff tonight?"

"You will see," I repeated.

I saw her watching me out the corner of my eye, and it made me smile.

Even after everything, the confessions, telling her I loved her, and promising to help, she still had trust issues.

That was going to be put to an end.

I came to a stop in front of the sycamore tree shutting off the truck, hopping out, and going around to the passenger side to help Evan out. She stood there, her eyes glazing over as she stared at the tree.

"Baby, look at me," I commanded. Once I had her attention, I smiled at her, not saying another word. She watched as I grabbed a blanket out from behind my truck seat and took her hand. I walked us under the full branches of the old tree and laid out the blanket, sitting on it and pulling Evan down with me.

"What are you doing?" she whispered.

"We are taking your fucking life back."

Evan's eyes filled with tears, and she looked at me with torment and heartbreak all over her beautiful face.

"Tonight, under this fucking tree, you are getting your entire world back. No more hiding, baby. Just you and me and nothing between us. The only person you belong to is me, and I'm here. I am here to help you claw out of your darkness because you deserve some fucking happiness. I want to make you happy, baby doll."

The tears fell fast down her cheeks, her body shook with the sobs escaping from deep within her chest.

It wasn't her crying.

This was a cleansing.

Evan was cleansing her entire soul of the darkness she'd never escaped.

I gently removed her flip flops from her feet, setting them down. I removed my boots and socks and placed them beside her sandals and stood, taking Evan by the hands and standing her up. I pulled my shirt from my body, dropping it and then helping Evan from hers. She watched me as I reached around, unclasping her bra and letting it fall.

My eyes stayed fixed on her as I unbuttoned my jeans and slid them down my legs along with my boxer briefs, letting them pool at my feet. Reaching over, I mimicked the motion, sliding Evans jeans and panties down her legs and coming to rest in front of her on my knees.

"You deserve to be fucking worshipped, Evan," I rasped, circling my arms around her thighs, bringing her closer to me until her bare pussy was at eye level. I could smell her arousal, and my mouth watered. I looked up to find Evan watching me.

"Keep your eyes on mine," I demanded. She nodded as I dipped my head and flicked my tongue over her clit. Her legs spasmed, and I held her closer. Spreading her legs farther apart, I flattened my tongue, taking one full lick of her entire pussy.

My eyes never left hers.

She watched as I began to devour her cunt, lapping her juices and biting her clit. Her eyes were glazed, and her mouth was open, her moans carrying on the night wind. I slowly pushed a finger in her and worked it in and out as I sucked on her lips and licked through her folds. I felt her inner walls tighten, and I knew she was close.

I stopped, pulling away.

"Come down here," I told her, still sitting on my knees. She lowered herself in front of me until she was resting on her knees, as well.

"What do you want, Evan?" I asked, reaching my hand out and circling one of her perfect, pink nipples with the finger that was still coated with her slickness.

"I don't know."

"You do, so tell me what you want," I repeated.

"I... I want it to all go away. Make me forget, Levi, please," she pleaded.

I took her face in my hands and softly kissed her.

"I'm yours, Evan. All yours. Everything we do here tonight is us claiming you. Claiming us. That's why I brought us here so you could remind yourself that no one but us matters."

CHAPTER TWENTY-TWO

EVAN

Us.

Levi and me.

We were all that mattered.

His words were the most beautiful words I had ever heard, and he meant every syllable.

He was mine, and I was his.

"Lay back," Levi commanded, his voice no more than a husky whisper. I did as he told me.

Levi leaned forward, bringing his lips to my thighs, kissing a light path up the length of my body. I had no thoughts of shame, no idea of being undeserving or dirty. All I was thinking of was this man and the emotions he was dragging out of me. One emotion in particular.

Hope.

Hope for real love, acceptance, and moving on.

He hovered over me, his eyes fixed on mine.

"I love you, and nothing is going to change that," Levi murmured.

"I love you," I replied back, fighting the tears away. No more crying. This night was about us, about me reclaiming the life I let be stolen the night my innocence was. I had given that man too much, and it was time I stopped letting him take even after he was dead and gone.

Levi spread my legs gently, bringing himself to rest between them. I could feel his hardness pressing against my wet folds, and I moved my hands down to his ass, pulling him to me. He took my lips, softly kissing me, whispering over and over that he loved me and that I was his and he was mine as he slid into me.

There was nothing rough about it. This was actual lovemaking. Something I had never allowed in my world.

Lazily pulling out and sliding back in over and over, Levi loved me under the stars as the fireflies floated around us, and the moon watched our act of beauty. Because that is what it was.

It was so fucking beautiful.

He was beautiful.

This man with the calloused hands and tattoos adorning his masculine figure was all the beauty in my life.

I needed him and wanted him.

And, I had him.

Levi continued his slow and steady rhythm, continually kissing my lips as my hips met his with each gentle thrust.

"Evan," he whispered, biting at my bottom lip as I felt the tightening in my belly. My orgasm rolled through me, a quiet wave I rode out as Levi began to come inside of me. I could feel him throbbing, and I felt the fullness as he emptied into me.

And, I had never felt happier.

We spent a couple hours out there, laying in each other's arms, watching the sky. The light breeze that rolled through rustled the leaves in the giant tree that loomed over us. I had never felt more loved than at that moment.

Levi loved me.

This man with his own dark past understood me, and I knew deep within my heart he was the one who would help me heal.

As we lay wrapped around one another, I told him just about everything. I told him about my resentment towards my mom, and how I had wished I could live with my aunt instead. I told him about dabbling with alcohol and drugs to forget my fucked up past. I told him about not wanting to fall for him and how I had failed miserably.

And, I told him I loved him.

I loved him body, mind, and broken soul.

Levi left the next morning, promising to return that evening after he took care of a few things. When I asked him what he meant he once again told me the less I knew, the better.

I decided I didn't want to know.

I traveled into town, stopping by the market for a few things before heading home. Grabbing what I needed, I headed for a check-out line. I placed my groceries on the belt and walked up to the credit card machine to be greeted by Hilda, one of Aunt Polly's friends.

"Evan! How are you sweetheart?" she asked as she scanned my things.

"I'm good, Hilda. How are you?"

"Just fine," Hilda replied, her German accent barely traceable. "Did you hear there is a substitute teacher position open over at the high school?"

"Really?"

"Yes, so I hope you don't mind, but I gave your number to my daughter. She works in the office."

I smiled wide. "No, Hilda." I laughed. "I don't mind, at all. Thank you so much for thinking of me."

"Of course, dear," she said as she finished ringing me up.

Not long after leaving the store, I pulled into my driveway, looking across the road to see if Levi was home yet. He wasn't. Getting out of my car, I unloaded the few bags of groceries I had and walked up the front porch, pulling the screen door open and turning the knob of the front door. As I walked in, I left the door open, letting the breeze from outside carry in through the screen.

I was putting my groceries away in the refrigerator when I heard a familiar voice.

"What's it like?"

I jumped at the sudden interruption. Slamming the door to the fridge shut, I looked up to find Della standing in the entryway. She was pale, a light sheen of sweat on her forehead. Her clothes were too big for her sunken frame, and she had nothing but old flip flops on her dirty feet.

"Della, you scared me," I said as I backed up, closing in on the knife block on the counter. I wasn't sure what she was capable of after our last run in. She had been angry and agitated, and I couldn't tell what her current mood was. She looked like she was deep in thought as she watched me.

"I'm sorry. I didn't mean to. I just didn't think you would let me in after how awful I was the last time I saw you."

"Why were you so pissed when you saw me, Della?" I asked.

She stood there, and if I hadn't been studying her face, I would have missed the single tear that traveled down her hollow cheek.

She wasn't here to hurt me, and I knew that as sure as I breathed.

"Come in, Della. Come sit and eat something, okay?" I offered.

She hesitated at first, but then she hung her head and walked into the kitchen, sitting at the small table as I got her a glass of water.

"Thank you," she whispered as I handed it to her. She grabbed my hand before I could pull it away, and my eyes met hers.

"Evan, why didn't you come back?"

It was the same thing she had asked the first time I saw her, and something told me she had an idea of why.

"I think you know why, don't you?" I said, sitting down in the chair next to her.

She held onto my hand as she nodded.

"Because of him," she whispered.

"Yes," I confirmed, squeezing her cold hand. "What happened, Della. What did he do?"

Della was quiet for what seemed like ages, her eyes staring at nothing. At first, I thought she hadn't heard me and was in the middle of some drug stupor. Then, she began to speak.

"Do you remember the last summer you and I had hung out?"

I told her I did.

"After you went home, I met a few older boys. They were the cool kids, you know. The bad boys all the girls liked. Well, anyway, I started hanging out with them, smoking weed and cigarettes because I wanted to be part of their crowd," she began. "Well, one night three of us were all behind the market, and the guys were tagging the place. Sheriff Sutton caught them. He arrested everyone and drove us to the station. I thought for sure I was going to be dead when my parents found out, but the sheriff came and got me and told me he was taking me home."

Her grip tightened on my hand, and her eyes glistened with unshed tears.

"I was so happy. I remember thinking he wasn't such a bad guy, and I didn't know why you hated him so much. So, I'm sitting in the passenger seat of his patrol car, and I thought he was driving so slow and taking the long way around. Then, he said he could tell my parents and get me in a world of trouble," she swallowed hard and continued, "or that it could be our secret. He pulled off onto a small dirt road and turned off the lights. I asked him what he was doing, and he asked me if I wanted to keep my criminal activities between us. I was fourteen fucking years old. Of course, I didn't want my parents to know, so I said I wanted to keep it between us."

I realized I had been holding my breath because I knew where this was going.

"He reached over and placed his hand on my thigh," Della whispered. "I was wearing a jean skirt my mom had just bought me for school; it had buttons all the way up the front. I realized he was unbuttoning them. I just remember freezing, not knowing what to do because I didn't want to get in trouble, and he was the sheriff! He... he put a finger inside my underwear and began to play with me. I started crying, and he told me there was nothing to cry about. Then, he pushed his finger in me. I closed my eyes, and when I opened them, he had his pants opened and was jerking himself as he..." she trailed off as the sobs overtook her. I was crying with her. The story she told me hit too close to home.

"You don't have to say anymore, Della," I told her, still holding her hand. She took a few deep breaths, and her eyes met mine.

"You don't get it, Evan. He held this over me for almost a year. That shit went on for almost a year!"

At that moment, it dawned on me why Della stopped talking to me.

"You stopped talking to me because you were trying to get away from him," I realized.

160

Della nodded.

"Towards the end, I figured out getting high all the time helped zone it all out, but before I knew it, I couldn't stop. Not weed, either. It wasn't enough. Coke and meth, mostly meth. And here I am, a fucking low-life failure," she spat.

I didn't know what to say.

Della had been my closest friend in Kendrick, and that man had ruined her life. He had taken her innocence and brought a bright and happy girl to her knees.

He'd destroyed her.

"Della," I said, getting her attention. She looked up at me with big, blue, haunted and hollow eyes, and I saw my friend in that one look. She was still in there.

I told her what had happened to me, what Louis had done to me, leaving out the part that Polly had killed him. I didn't know how to tell her that.

"Evan, that piece of shit has been out there for almost twenty years. Think of all the other girls he's done this to," she cried.

"Look at me, Della," I commanded, my voice strong. When I had her attention, I lowered my head, meeting her eyes. "Louis Sutton never touched another girl after the night he raped me, understand?"

Della looked at me with confusion on her once pretty face.

"He never touched another girl," I repeated, and I saw the moment my meaning registered.

Della took a deep breath, looking to the ceiling and closing her eyes.

Looking back to me, she whispered, " I fucking hope he is rotting deep in hell."

CHAPTER TWENTY-THREE

EVAN

"Evan!" I heard Levi shout as the front porch screen slammed behind him.

The sound of his deep, gruff voice made me smile.

"In here!" I called out from the kitchen where I was putting together a spaghetti dinner. I watched as Levi entered the kitchen, and my heart stopped beating for what had to be an entire second. I never believed in all of that shit about a man changing the course of some love-struck woman's life, but this man? This man had done just that.

The screen slammed again, and I knew instantly who'd followed behind Levi.

"God damn, what the fuck smells so good?" Rex bellowed as he clomped down the hall.

Rex sauntered into the kitchen wearing a pair of dirty work boots, cut-off camouflaged cargo pants, and a grease-stained, tight white tank top. His hair was pulled back into a low ponytail, and the craziest part of the whole thing was he made the look work.

"I made a spaghetti dinner, so I hope you guys want to stay," I smiled at them.

Levi came across the kitchen, wrapping his arms around me and kissing me. I would never get tired of his mouth.

"So," Rex interrupted, "when's dinner?"

The ceiling creaked under the footsteps of the person upstairs. Levi pulled back from me, looking up towards the sound.

"Lucy here?" he asked.

"No," I started, but before I could say any more the creak made its way down the stairs, and Della appeared in the kitchen.

No one said a word as Levi and Rex looked at Della, surprise on both of their faces.

"What the fuck is she doing here?" Levi asked, his voice raised.

"Levi," I began, wanting to explain, but Della spoke up.

"I came here to ask Evan about the molesting she went through by the hands of that pedophile fuck. The same pedophile fuck that molested me. We talked, and she let me shower and gave me some clean clothes. I called my mom, and I am going to have dinner here. Then, she is taking me to my parents' house because I am ready to get clean. Does that explain everything enough, or do you have any other questions?" Della challenged.

Neither Rex nor Levi said a word, but a small smirk appeared on Rex's lips.

Della sounded like the girl I had known so many years ago. She was fun and sassy when we were kids, but to look at the shell standing in front of me, you would never know.

Her once athletic body was now lanky, the muscles replaced with skin and bone. Her long, blonde hair limp and lifeless, wet from the shower and hanging around her shoulders. I could still see the carefree, beautiful girl trapped inside of her, clawing to get out.

And Della would break her free, I just knew it.

I drove Della to her parents' home across town after what could be called an awkward dinner. Levi barely spoke, and Rex openly stared at Della. When she would catch him and their eyes would meet, she quickly looked away. Rex did not.

We pulled into the two-story home in one of the small neighborhoods in town that Mr. and Mrs. Richardson moved to after selling their home to Levi.

Della moved to open the door of my car, and I grabbed her wrist before she could get out. She looked at me for a moment.

"Get help, Della," I told her, my voice quiet.

She smiled as she pulled her arm away. "I'm ready, Evan. I really am. I can't live like this anymore. And honestly, tonight was what I needed to move past all the bad shit I went through."

She said nothing else as she got out. I looked out the front windshield and saw her mom waiting at the front door. When Della walked up, they embraced, Mrs. Richardson pulling back and grasping Della's face in her palms, crying. The two women stood there for a moment looking at each other. I could see her mom's lips moving, and I watched as Della nodded before they went inside.

The broken, drug-addicted Della was about to disappear, and the beautiful and free-spirited Della would reappear. I would put money on it.

CHAPTER TWENTY-FOUR

LEVI

Seeing Della Richardson standing in Evan's house pissed me the fuck off. That girl was seriously messed up, and I didn't want her around. But, when she told me why she had come, and why she came to Evan, I wanted nothing more than to let her stay and help her.

That worthless fucker had put his hands on her, too.

Della didn't go into detail, but she didn't need to. The sadness that had followed her around for so many years was proof enough.

But tonight, there was something different in those methed-out eyes. Determination.

I hoped to fuck she got herself the help she needed. The Richardson's were good people and getting their daughter back was something they needed.

When Evan returned from dropping Della at her parents', she came over to my house, walking up the front porch and sitting next to me. The night was warm, the summer winding down. These types of nights were something people wrote fucking novels about.

"We're moving him tomorrow night," I told Evan, taking a drink from my beer.

She didn't say anything at first, something about Evan I fucking loved. She didn't fill the silence with worthless chatter but instead saved her words for shit that mattered.

"Okay, do you need my help?"

"No, like I said before, the less you know, the better. We got this handled," I said.

Evan nodded her head as she stared out across the field at her own home.

"That could have been you," I said, thinking out loud.

Evan looked at me. "What do you mean?"

"Della. That could have easily been you."

"Levi, the same stuff happened to both of us," she said, not understanding just what I was saying.

"Yeah, I know that. But, the way she coped with all of it that could have been you. The drugs and shit. But, you didn't go down that fucking hole, Evan. You're stronger than you let yourself believe, baby doll. So fucking strong."

Evan laughed, shaking her head.

"You honestly don't know, Levi. I wasn't strong."

I looked at her, trying to read what was going through that gorgeous head of hers, but the woman gave away nothing.

"I coped other ways," was all she said.

"Are you going to fill me in? No secrets, remember?" I reminded her.

"Yeah, I remember. Are you sure you really want to know?"

"Yep," I answered. And, I did want to know.

"Okay, fine," she started, "I coped by fucking just about every man who was ever nice to me, trying to find someone who would just love me. But you know what that got me? Nothing. Not even a second date or phone call. When I met you, I promised myself I wouldn't sleep with you, but that didn't work. So, now that you know your new girlfriend is a murdering whore, are you having second thoughts?"

I didn't answer right away, thinking about Evan so fucking lonely that she would let any asshole put his dick in her pissed me off. But not because she fucked them, but because they fucked her.

"You're quiet," Evan said, breaking me from my thoughts.

I grabbed her hand, getting her attention. Taking her face in my hands, I kissed her lightly and rested my forehead against hers.

"Evan, nothing changes. Nothing fucking changes. Those guys meant shit, and that's all they were. Pieces of shit who used you. All that's over, baby. You're mine, don't you get that?"

Evan pulled back a little, sitting up and looking back out to the field.

"You know, I think my aunt knew exactly what she was doing by bringing me here," she said, pulling her knees up and wrapping her arms around them.

"Why do you say that?" I asked.

"Not sure, but somehow that woman knew you and I were right. She knew you were what I needed. I don't think she knew you were the right guy to move the dead body on her property, but if she was still here with all of this happening, I think she would have come to you to help her."

"I think you're right," I agreed, smiling at the thought of Polly. "She told me once that you and I were going to make a good couple one day."

Evan turned her head, her eyes meeting mine, and the look on her face made me laugh.

"She really said that?" Evan asked.

I nodded my head as I took another swig of beer.

"What the fuck? She never even told me about you or Rex. Can you believe that?"

"She was a woman of mystery, that is for sure," I chuckled as Evan pouted. "But, she was also a smart woman who knew what the hell she was talking about, you know why?"

Evan smiled. "Nope, tell me."

"Because she was right. You and I are good together. We belong together, baby doll, and I want to keep you forever."

*

The next night Rex drove my truck, and I drove the mini excavator out to the back of Evan's property. She had shown me the general location of where they had buried the body, so once out there, I began a slow dig of the area. Evan thought they had dug pretty deep, but knowing the tractor Polly had used, he couldn't be more than four feet underground.

Rex kept the spotlights on the area as he downed a beer, throwing the empty bottle in the hole I was digging. What the fuck did it matter? Once we pulled the body out, the land was no longer our concern.

It took a while, digging out one large area, before I saw the blue tarp. I stopped digging, shutting off the machine, hopping down and walking to the edge of the hole.

"There he is," Rex said, another beer in hand.

"Yep."

Without saying a word, we both spit on Louis Sutton's dead fucking body.

"You call Skinner?" I asked Rex, standing there staring down at the blue piece of plastic.

"Yeah, he said to text him when we have him loaded. He'll get a few guys together and meet us. Said it's all good."

Skinner was an acquaintance of Rex's, and the guy we called when we needed help with something we didn't want to dirty our hands with. He was a little fucking off, and that was being kind.

Skinner was a fucking lunatic.

We had met with Skinner the night before, and the way his eyes lit up when we told him what we needed made my fucking skin crawl.

That was why they called him Skinner.

I didn't want to think of what the guys he was getting to help him were like.

Skinner was tall and gaunt. His face was long, and his black hair hung in greasy strings. I had never seen him in anything but dirty jeans, a chain wallet, old, worn-out Nikes and a Bud Lite T-shirt with a hole in the collar. I knew how much we had paid him in the past, so it was a mystery as to why he didn't have other clothes.

"What are you going to do with him?" Rex had asked as Skinner lit a hand-rolled cigarette.

"Oh, I got a guy. I'm fairly certain there'll still be some meat on the bones, so I'm dropping him off to let the beetles eat him. They'll clean him right up."

"Okayyyyyyy," Rex started, "what exactly are you going to do with clean bones?"

Skinner looked at Rex like he asked him the most fucked up thing he had ever heard.

"I'm gonna sell 'em. What the fuck else would I do with them? I can make a pretty penny off those fucking clean bones on the dark web."

Fuck. I wished Rex hadn't asked. I could only imagine what kind of sick fuck wanted to buy human bones.

As I dug out around the tarp, I was careful not to put any pressure on the body. Once I had dug out enough, I backed the machine up and let Rex jump down into the hole. He tied a rope around the outside of the tarp, crossing it back and forth around the body, binding it so the tarp wouldn't come apart.

Jumping out of the hole, Rex walked over to the bucket on the excavator, knotting the other end of the rope to it. After he was done, he gave me the thumbs up, and I started inching back, slowly pulling the tarp out of the hole. I saw blue slide up and onto the ground, and I stopped, turning the machine off and jumping down.

"I'll get the truck," I said.

Rex and I pulled the body up and into the back of my truck using the rope. I covered it with some of the dirt I had dug out, hiding it from view. No one was going to stop or question me, but precautions were never a bad idea.

I had called Brendan that morning, filling him in on the night's events. Having the town sheriff in on the transport and sale of a rotting corpse would be beneficial.

He let his deputy have the night off, telling him he needed to be home with his wife and new baby and clearing the road for Rex and me.

No one would be bothering us tonight.

Rex and I drove out through Lancaster, taking rural route six and turning off on the old service road that led to the water tower. This was where we had planned our meet and greet with Skinner and his band of dirtbags.

I shut the headlights off as we slowly drove. The moon was so bright that we could clearly see the road. I saw Skinner's old Ford, complete with his camper, and came to a stop. The fucker lived in that camper, and I was pretty sure he had nowhere to put the body but in there.

Yeah. The fucker was demented.

"You think he's putting that in there?" Rex asked, staring at the beat up old truck and camper.

"Oh, fuck yeah. Where the hell else is he going to put it?"

"I think he cooks meth in there, too," Rex told me.

"Let's get this shit over with," I replied, and I fucking meant it. Being around Skinner always made me want to take a shower in bleach.

Rex got out and walked over to the driver's side window of Skinner's truck. I could see the cloud of smoke that came out when he rolled the window down, even in the darkness. I turned my truck around and backed it up to Skinner's, turning the engine off and getting out to join Rex.

Skinner got out of his truck, and from the passenger side, two more men appeared. These two looked even dirtier than Skinner.

One of the guys was a damn kid, no more than sixteen. He was tall and lanky, and his jeans looked like they were about to fall off him.

The other was older with the same black, stringy hair as Skinner and almost as tall.

"My boy and my brother," Skinner pointed with his smoke.

A fucking family business.

"They cool with all this?" Rex asked, eyeing both of them.

"Fuck yeah, they're cool. My brother's the one who got all them beetles, and my boy there is the one who gets on the interwebs and sells this shit for me. We like to keep business in the family. Can't trust outsiders," Skinner stated.

"We're outsiders," I pointed out.

"Well, you are, but Rex is like family," Skinner replied.

"No, we're not," Rex argued, shaking his head and crossing his arms over his chest.

I laughed at his reaction.

"Yes," Skinner declared, "we are."

"Oh, fuck no we're not. We are business acquaintances. Nothing fucking more, and let's get this business done," Rex commanded, and I couldn't agree more.

We watched as the kid and Skinner's brother pulled the tarp from the dirt in the back of my truck and dumped it on the ground. Neither of them seemed phased one bit that they were hauling a dead body around in the middle of the night on an abandoned road. Skinner barked orders to them as he watched.

They lifted the tarp, the kid on one end and the brother on the other. Just as we thought, they took it around Skinner's truck and put it in the fucking camper. Neither of them spoke as the kid shut the door to the camper. They both got back in the passenger side of the truck, leaving Rex and me alone with Skinner.

He turned to me and held out his hand.

"My two grand, please," he said, snapping his fingers.

I pulled the rolled-up money out of my back pocket and handed it over, watching as he unwound the wad and counted. When he seemed satisfied, he smiled, his yellow teeth shining in the moonlight.

"It's always a pleasure doing business with you two. I like your money."

"We like your services," Rex answered.

Nodding, Skinner replied, "I know."

The filthy fucker turned away and got in his truck, starting the loud engine and pulling away from us.

"Why is that guy so fucking creepy?" Rex asked.

"I don't know. I mean, he is your family, so shouldn't you know?" I laughed and got in my truck to leave.

When we got back to my place, Rex took off for home, leaving me to head over to Evan's house. It was a little past one in the morning, but her lights were still on, and I promised her I would come over after everything was taken care of.

I reached for my cell and dialed Brendan as I walked over.

"Hello?" he answered.

"It's me. Everything is good, and I'm home. Thanks for your help tonight."

"No problem, man. Is Evan all good?"

"Heading there now, but I think she will be," I told him as I headed up her front porch, stopping at the door.

"That fuck Skinner get out of town?"

"Yep, he's gone."

"Good. I don't like that guy being here. I got the stuff you need. I can bring it by tomorrow. I'll talk to you later."

I laughed as I hung up. Brendan hated Skinner, but he knew he was harmless. Skinner got rid of the shit no one else wanted to touch, and he did it happily.

That was probably why Brendan didn't like him.

He got off on some sick shit.

176

CHAPTER TWENTY-FIVE

EVAN

The light knocks at my front door startled me, but I knew it was Levi. He was back from doing whatever it was he did with the body.

I swung the front door opened and was greeted by the smile of the man who had pulled me out of my self-induced hell and showed me what real love was. He was standing there, hands in his pockets, looking so fucking sexy I could barely stand it.

"Hey," I quietly said as I unlatched the screen door.

Levi walked in, shutting and locking the door behind him. He wrapped his strong arms around me and pulled me to him, making me feel safe and loved.

"You good?" he asked, looking down at me, his face full of concern.

"I'm fine," I laughed. "Are you good?"

"Yep, all good. Let's go upstairs and take a shower. I feel fucking disgusting."

"Why? What happened?" I questioned, worried something had gone wrong.

Levi smiled and tapped the end of my nose. "Need to know, remember?"

"Yes, I remember, and I also remember that you feel disgusting and want a shower," I teased.

He motioned for me to go first.

"After you."

We showered, taking our time and talking as we washed each other's backs. Levi spent a little longer washing mine, telling me my ass cheeks needed to be extra clean and making me laugh.

"Tell me about your summers here before everything happened," he urged as we stood under the warm stream of water.

"They were the best times of my childhood. Coming here was magical to me, and I loved it."

"Kendrick? Magical?" Levi laughed.

"Yes, asshole! To a kid being here is a magic place. My summers were spent traveling to the farmers market and watching my aunt talk to the Amish people. Helping her sell her produce after we picked it. Being able to run around barefoot and catch fireflies at night with her and swimming in the criver during the day. Running back and forth between our house and Della's, and riding bikes down the gravel road and not worrying one bit about someone taking us. This place twenty-five years ago was amazing."

" I guess this place is still pretty magical. I mean, you're here," he said, smiling.

Levi had a way of making me love him more and more with every look, and those smiles locked me in as his forever.

"I wanted to live with her," I told him. "I loved my mom, still do, but I had a bond with Aunt Polly that I didn't with my mom. I don't know how to explain it."

"She was your hero," Levi said.

"Yeah," I smiled, thinking of her. "She was my hero. Polly was the strongest woman I have ever known. I remember not understanding why she married him, but I think I finally figured it out."

And I had. Aunt Polly had me every summer, and she had her friends the rest of the year, but at night when she returned home, she was alone.

"She didn't want to be alone forever."

Deep down, I had always known why she married the sheriff who seemed so nice. The man she knew nothing about. She wanted someone in her life to come home to at night, someone to love her all year long.

"That woman never needed to worry about being alone. Everyone in this town adored her," Levi reassured me. "She needed a man in her life, and she settled. That's what happened, baby doll. She settled for the first man who paid attention to her in a very long time."

"What makes you say that?"

Levi smiled one of those clit throbbing smiles.

"She told me."

Levi turned the water off, and we got out of the shower. We went into my room and got dressed, me in light cotton sleep shorts and a cami and Levi in a pair of actual boxer shorts. It was warm out, so we got a carton of chocolate ice cream out of the freezer and two spoons and sat on the front porch swing. The fireflies were out, lazily floating around the front yard and the fields, making the scene surreal and beautiful.

After the last few weeks' events, my confessions to Levi, Della's confession to me, and the removal of the dead body I helped bury in my backyard, I found it odd I had never been happier.

Content for the first time in my life. And, I was sitting next to the man who brought me that.

"I love you, Levi Kincaid. I love you, and I don't even know your middle name," I laughed as he pulled me into him, kissing me on the top of my head.

"It's James. Levi James Kincaid," he told me.

"Well, Levi James Kincaid, I love you."

"I love you, baby doll," he responded, his arm around me as we sat side by side.

The next morning, I woke up to find my bed empty, which it hadn't been when I fell asleep after a session of mind-blowing sex. Levi never ceased to amaze me with the tricks and surprises he pulled out in the bedroom.

I dressed quickly and headed downstairs to find him in the kitchen, making breakfast. Or, his idea of breakfast at least. He had made us protein shakes, and the thick concoction was sitting in a large glass on my counter. Levi stood in the middle of the kitchen, his glorious body on display in nothing but those fucking boxer shorts, as he gulped down his shake. When he saw me, he put his glass down and smiled.

"Morning," he drawled.

"Hey, I woke up lonely." I made my best pouty face, but all it got me was a laugh.

"Sorry, I'm an early riser. You should know that by now."

"I do, but I was hoping I could coax you into staying in bed with me today," I teased.

"Evan, you don't need to try to coax me. I will happily stay in bed with you. Any day but today; I have something I need to get today."

I pouted harder, making sad, puppy dog eyes as I sat down.

"Nice try," Levi said before he gulped down the rest of his shake. "I won't be gone all day. How about that?"

I stuck my tongue out and panted like a dog, nodding my head vigorously, making him laugh again.

"Jesus, you're impossible." Levi chuckled.

After Levi left, I found myself alone and lonely. I had gone from being a woman who was okay with being the loner to a woman who couldn't imagine being alone. Levi, Rex, Lucy, even Della had become my people. People I adored and wanted to be around, and I had Aunt Polly to thank for it.

I still hadn't done anything with her ashes. I didn't know what to do with them, really. I did know she didn't deserve to be shoved in a tiny urn stuck on her mantel.

I walked into the living room and took the urn from above the fireplace.

"Thank you," I whispered, kissing the side of the silver container.

I fully believed my aunt knew exactly what she was doing when she fired Lucy and asked for me to come back to Kendrick to care for her. She knew Levi was right for me, and she knew coming back here would give me the closure to a terrible chapter in my life, one I should have closed long ago but was too wrapped up in my own self-pity that I wouldn't turn the page.

I had more than turned the page.

I'd thrown that fucking book in a fire and burned it.

*

The following day I walked out to the back of the property, the old sycamore standing tall against the afternoon sky. I could see where Levi had dug out the body, the hole freshly refilled with dirt. I wondered what the workers would think when they saw it. Would they assume right away that my aunt had killed a man and buried him on her property? The thought made me laugh. No one would have ever thought Aunt Polly was capable of any such thing.

She was a saint.

I stood for a moment, looking up at the tree that had meant so much to me as a kid and held my darkest secret as an adult.

"You don't have to hide it for me anymore," I said out loud. I approached the trunk of the tree, placing my hand on the bark and tracing the lines as I walked around it.

I was saying goodbye.

I turned and pressed my back against it, sliding down to sit on the ground. Closing my eyes, I could see Aunt Polly sitting there with me, handing me a sandwich and quietly eating side by side in the shade.

Opening my eyes, I took in the beauty that was all around me. I was where I belonged.

A few days passed since Levi and Rex dug up Louis from under the sycamore tree. Things had returned to normal, whatever that might be. I wasn't sure if life in Kendrick would ever be classified as normal.

I was just walking into the kitchen from my back patio when I heard the knock at my front door. I quickly walked to the door, swinging it wide to be surprised by who stood on the other side.

"Mrs. Richardson," I exclaimed, smiling.

"Hello Evan, and please, call me Diane."

I nodded my head. "Would you like to come in?" I asked, stepping back and holding the door open with my body.

"Thank you," Diane said as she stepped inside.

I shut the screen door, leaving the front door open in case Levi showed up.

"I don't mean to intrude, and I'll only take a minute," she said as she followed me into the kitchen.

"No worries, Diane. It's nice to see you. Do you want anything to drink?" I asked.

"No, I'm good, Evan. I just needed to say thank you."

"For?"

Diane smiled, tears forming in her eyes.

"For giving me my daughter back. She told me everything, and I am so sorry, Evan. I am so sorry for what happened to you."

"Diane, there's nothing to be sorry about. You didn't know."

"I wish I did, though. I lost so many years with Della because of that bastard, and I had no clue. I feel like the worst mother," she cried. "I understand why you never came back."

The tears were rushing down her face in a cascade of grief, the hurt in her eyes more than I could take.

"But I'm back now, and I'm not going anywhere. I'm here, and I plan on staying," I told her.

It took her a moment to get herself back under control as she took deep breaths to stop her sobs.

"Polly knew you would end up settling here. She always knew."

I laughed. "My aunt knew me more than I understood."

"Polly knew more than most of us," Diane agreed. "I miss her; she was a good friend. Kind of like the friend you are to Della. You know? People in this town who have known my girl her entire life would look the other way when she came around, not wanting to be bothered with the trouble that came with her. But you? You didn't shy away when she came to you for help. That was a very Polly thing to do."

"I wonder why Della never went to my aunt," I wondered out loud.

"She did. Polly is who helped us place Della in her first rehab, but Della left after only a week into the treatment. She never asked Polly for anything again after that."

"Something in Della's eyes told me she was ready to get her life back the day she came to me. I think this time is it," I reassured Diane.

She smiled. "Me, too."

Diane hugged me tightly and promised to invite Levi and me over for dinner to celebrate when Della finished her rehab.

I told her we would be there, and I couldn't wait.

I truly meant it.

CHAPTER TWENTY-SIX

EVAN

Levi returned to my house later that day, carrying a newspaper in his hand. He smiled wide as he saw me sitting on the porch swing, and I couldn't help but smile back.

"Hey, baby doll," he said as he walked up the steps and sat beside me. I scooted closer, turning my body so I could wrap my arms around him. "I can get used to this kind of greeting," he teased, pulling me close and kissing me.

He smelled good, like a clean summer breeze and pine, and I loved it.

"So, get used to it because I don't think I'm ever going to stop greeting you like this," I told him. "What do you have there?"

He held the newspaper up and shook it.

"You mean this?"

I rolled my eyes.

"Yes, that."

He scooted away from me and opened the paper, making a show of holding it up to his face pretending to read. It said 'The Verde Independent' on it.

"What paper is that?" I asked him, squinting my eyes to read.

"Sedona, Arizona," he answered, still reading through the paper.

"Arizona? Why did you get that? And how?"

"It's a few days old. I had someone send it to me."

Why would he have someone send him a newspaper from Arizona?

I sat and glared at him, waiting for a better explanation as he thumbed through the pages.

"Here it is," he announced, shaking the paper to fold the pages back. He leaned over, handing the paper to me. I took it from his hands and glanced at it, not sure what I was supposed to be looking at.

Levi placed his finger on it, and my breath caught.

The obituary section.

The obituary for Louis Sutton.

I looked up, my eyes seeking out an answer from Levi.

"No more worrying, Evan. It's all taken care of," he assured me.

"How?" I asked, my heart racing as I looked back to the paper.

"I have friends. We have friends," Levi said. "Brendan called in a few favors from a couple computer nerds he knows, and this is the outcome."

I stared at the small blip in the obituary section of the paper for Louis Sutton.

No picture, no next of kin, no listing of a funeral.

Just a generic blurb regarding an old man who died alone.

It was more than he deserved.

A heavy weight lifted off me as I read the small, insignificant obituary.

This cleared any sort of doubt anyone may have had regarding the disappearance of Louis. It cleared any speculation of my aunt and her involvement.

This cleared my worry of being caught.

"Thank you," I whispered.

"Evan, there are people in this world that no one misses when they disappear. Louis was one of those people," Levi said.

"I always wonder why he chose my aunt to prey on," I wondered out loud.

"He chose her because she was beautiful and alive, and men like that want to feed off it. You being here was an added bonus. The guy was a predator in every way, Evan," Levi answered. "He was never missed. No one asked about him, and no one ever will."

**

The clearing of the land began the following morning. By midafternoon, the sycamore tree was gone, and the dirt was leveled. The property looked naked and exposed without that giant tree looming in the distance, and I felt like I had lost a confidante.

Levi and I stood in the distance watching as the landscape changed.

"Rex and I will get out here and get the barbed wire fence back up," he offered.

"It looks so wrong without that tree back here," I said as I watched the commotion in front of me.

"Don't worry, baby doll. We'll think of something, okay?"

Levi always seemed to know what to say to me and when I needed to hear it.

He knew me.

And, I needed someone to know me.

Weeks passed, and fall was here. The days were already getting shorter, the nights cooler. Levi spent every night with me, only going home to shower and get his equipment to head off to work.

I loved the normalcy of it all.

He would come home after work, and we would cook dinner and clean up.

We would sit out on the porch swing and talk about our days.

We would hold hands and walk along the property.

We would make love before falling asleep in each other's arms.

We would wake up to the alarm and shower together before heading downstairs to have coffee and send Levi off to work.

It was boring, and I loved every second of it.

One night, Levi's phone rang on the bedside table. He grunted as he reached over me to answer it.

Who the hell was calling in the middle of the night? One guess.

"What?" Levi growled into the phone. He listened for a minute with his eyes closed.

"Fuck, alright. I'll be there," he said before hanging up.

"What's going on?" I asked, my eyes heavy with sleep.

"I need to go help Rex and Brendan with something," he answered.

"Rex and Brendan hate each other," I pointed out.

"Yeah, yeah they do. But not when it comes to the wife beater Brendan just arrested."

"If he arrested him, why does he need you and Rex?"

"Because, baby doll, Brendan can't get his hands dirty."

What did that mean?

"Look, Brendan is a good man, and even a good man knows sometimes you have to do not so good things to keep shit safe. Rex and I assist him with that."

"Is this another instance where the less I know, the better?" I asked, already knowing the answer.

"Exactly," he said as he climbed out of bed and got dressed. "I shouldn't be too long, okay?"

"Okay."

I should have been worried. They were about to do something illegal and violent, and something told me they weren't new to this, at all.

But, I wasn't worried.

I was proud.

Levi.

My sweet, caring, quiet, and sensitive Levi was someone people feared.

I had never felt so safe and warm in my life.

CHAPTER TWENTY-SEVEN

LEVI

Fucking Brendan. He knew I had a thing about piece-of-shit wife beaters. He knew Rex also had just as big a thing about beating the shit out of people.

He also knew he kept a lot of people safe with his not so legal methods.

The entire town knew, and not a single law-abiding citizen cared.

When I arrived at the sheriff's station, the guy was handcuffed and bleeding from his head.

His clothes were covered in dirt and blood, and he was barely conscious.

Brendan sat across from him, and Rex stood in the corner of the small office area, his cell to his ear.

"So?" I asked Brendan.

"He's my brother in law," he answered.

"Oh fuck, man. Really?"

"Yeah. I saw my sister in town today, and I hugged her. She stiffened up like she was in pain and after asking and asking she finally showed me. Her fucking arms are covered in bruises," he told me, not taking his eyes off the man across from him.

"What do you want to do?"

"He's already agreed to divorce her and leave her half of everything. Rex helped him decide. I told him no charges," Brendan explained. "Rex is getting him his train ticket. He leaves tonight. I need you to drop his ass off."

"What about your sister?"

The bloody man came to, lifting his head at the mention of his wife. Brendan met his eyes and smiled.

"She'll be fine," was all he replied as he stared the guy down.

I dropped the guy off at the train station around two in the morning, not saying anything as he got out. Once he shut the door to my truck, I took off, leaving him there with a bloody face and a ticket in hand.

It may not have been the most political way to handle things, but it was effective.

It was hard to believe the brother in law of the town sheriff would pull something like that. The asshole had to be ten shades of stupid.

I called Brendan on my way back to Evan's.

"All good?" he asked.

"Yep."

"You know something?" he started. "You and Evan? The two of you will work. It's okay if you tell her about all of this."

No one ever really knew about the help Rex and I provided to Brendan, only speculation. We never killed anyone or anything like that, and he didn't call us that often. But we could persuade them to leave. One way or another.

It was usually Rex doing the persuading. I just did the driving.

"Why?" I asked.

"Because Evan was one of these people. Evan was one of these women we've helped. She'll understand. Fuck, she may even want to help."

No way was she getting involved in anything like this.

"Look, I'll tell her if she ever asks, but you are not to get her involved, you understand? She's been through enough shit in her life."

"I respect that," Brendan responded, and we ended the call.

I got back to Evan's and climbed into bed, pulling her warm body to me and closing my eyes.

I felt no guilt about what I had just helped with as I held her close and drifted off to sleep.

I woke to a small hand stroking my cock. Not a bad way to wake up. I opened my eyes and found Evan watching me.

"Good morning," I smiled, putting my hands behind my head.

She climbed on top of me and sank down on my hard cock.

"It's going to be a great morning," she said as she fucked me awake. I was going to have no problem getting used to this. Having this woman by my side and in my bed was all I had never known I wanted.

And so much more.

She was my fucking universe, and I would do anything for her.

Anything.

CHAPTER TWENTY-EIGHT

EVAN

Eight months later

Spring was in the air, and I found it hard to believe I had been in Kendrick for almost a year. I loved it here. It was home.

Levi had moved in with me, renting his house to Rex so he could keep the business there. Rex was not the best neighbor, coming over at all times and making himself at home. I secretly loved it, and Levi made it no secret that he didn't.

I had accepted a substitute teaching job at the high school, and I loved every second of it. The kids were assholes, and they didn't want to listen. When I got just one of those assholes to be excited about a book or an assignment, I felt I had done my job.

It was gratifying.

Della had completed rehab and was working at the little market in town. She seemed really happy there. She looked amazing and healthy, her hair had it's luster back, and her gaunt frame had filled out. She had taken up running, telling me most addicts needed another addiction after they kicked drugs.

"Most of us start smoking, but smoking grosses me out," she said. "Running is a much better addiction."

I would see her running everywhere, including down my road. Once in a while, she would stop in front of her old house and look at it before continuing on.

When I could, I would meet her at the end of my drive on her way back and invite her to come sit with me. She would always respond by telling me she would drive over later after she was done with her run.

The Della I knew was back, and it felt so good to see her again.

***

One evening, Levi pulled into our driveway and honked the horn. I came out onto the porch to find him climbing into the back of his truck.

"What are you doing?" I called out to him.

"I got you something," he called back as I heard him jump down from the bed and slide something out. I walked down the stairs and came around to the tailgate.

"It's an oak seedling," he said, "for the back of the property."

I smiled wide at him, wondering if it was possible to love him any more than I did.

"Levi, it's beautiful!" I exclaimed as I eyed the little tree he held. "This is the kindest thing anyone has ever done for me."

"Let's get it in the ground," he suggested, and an idea hit me.

"One second," I called over my shoulder as I ran back into the house. I came back out, holding Aunt Polly in my hands. "I know what to do with her ashes."

Levi drove us to the back of the property near the fence line he and Rex had put in for me. Rex even planted blackberry bushes along it, "To keep people off the property," he had told me.

Levi stopped the truck and got out, and I noticed the hole for the tree was already dug as I grabbed the urn and hopped out. He went to the bed of the truck and slid the tree to the end, lifting it out and carrying it over to the hole.

"When did you dig this?" I asked.

"Yesterday."

"Thank you. This will look perfect back here."

"I thought it would, too. Now, what's your plan for Polly?" he asked as I walked over to him, standing over the freshly dug hole. I smiled at him as I opened the lid and poured her ashes in it.

"I couldn't think of anything she would have loved more. She will always be part of this place and us," I said as I began to cry happy tears.

Levi and I sat together after we planted the tree, not saying a word as we watched the sun start setting and the first fireflies of spring sleepily make their way out of the ground. I could feel his stare on me, and I turned my head only to be met with the most beautiful steel gray eyes.

"Baby doll," he began, and I knew what was coming next. I answered before he could even get the words out.

"Yes."

Levi looked at me and smiled as he reached around to his back pocket and pulled out a tiny red box.

"You sure about that?" he asked.

"I've never been so sure about an answer in my life."

He opened the box, and I recognized the ring immediately. It had been my aunts. She had worn it as long as I could remember. It was old, with intricate etchings and a large ruby in the center. I had always loved that ring.

My mouth fell as he held it out to me.

"Where did you get that?" I asked.

"Lucy gave it to me, and Polly had given it to her. She knew, baby doll. Polly always knew it was you and me. She gave this to Lucy for me to propose to you with."

I felt a shiver run through my body, and a sudden calm took over.

Polly was still looking out for me.

"She was right. It is you and me. And, my answer still stands," I told him as he slipped the ring on my finger.

"Yes."

The End of Levi and Evans story...

SIGN UP

Join our Mailing List to be alerted of new Imperial Publishing House Releases: http://bit.ly/2Pu0D3U

Made in the USA
Middletown, DE
18 May 2019